The Midwife in the Middle

Jennifer Drewett

Acknowledgements

Just as it takes a village to raise a child, it takes support to write a book. I couldn't have written 'The Midwife in the Middle' without some key figures.

Lisa the manuscript evaluator, Laë the editor, Rachel the cover artist, and Paige the character artist did amazing work for 'The Midwife in the Middle' which wouldn't be as it is without any of you.

My best friend Jenny has been a cheerleader for Tegan's story to be written since I told her about Tegan 20 years ago. Much like Tegan's story, we've gone through a lot of phases through the years. I'm glad we've dealt with them together.

'The Midwife in the Middle' is dedicated to the neurodivergent folks who enjoy some romance on or off the page.

We exist and we're valid.

Content Warnings

In no particular order, here are the content warnings for 'The Midwife in the Middle':

- Drug references

- Fatphobia

- Violence

- Mentions of blood

- Harassment

- Pregnancies

- Bullying

- Infidelity

- Drinking alcohol/Intoxication

- Anxiety attack

- Self harm/neglect

- Discussion of murder

- Discussion of familial death

- Domestic abuse & violence

- Slut shaming

- Medical emergencies

- Police incompetence

Contents

Moving On

♥

The brightly coloured living room was a contrast to the darkening January day. The walls were covered in residue bits of blue tac where posters and pictures were previously held. They were laid neatly on the coffee table, stacked on top of each other. A ginger haired woman with freckles came from the spare bedroom into the living room with a suitcase in one hand and a packed sports bag in another. She looked at the posters and pictures: they held memories of a relationship that no longer existed. As she held them, the front door to the flat was unlocked from the outside. An auburn haired, plus sized woman came through the door and locked it behind her. She kicked her shoes off by the shoe rack but was stopped in her tracks by a couple of packed boxes in the hallway towards the spare bedroom with her name 'Tegan' on them. A pang of confusion and upset hit the auburn haired woman's heart.

"*That was bloody quick,*" Tegan thought to herself. "*I need more time.*"

"Felicity, darling, hurry up!" the ginger haired woman shouted from the living room, not truly aware of who was in the hallway. Tegan's upset turned into anger as she stormed into the room to find the ginger haired woman in her home.

"What are you doing in my home, Alicia?" Tegan demanded. Alicia turned to face Tegan, ready and raring for an argument.

"It's not exactly your home anymore, is it? It's mine and Felicity's." Alicia sneered. Tegan did her best to try and repress her rising anger: after all, Tegan didn't want to give Alicia what she wanted.

"Where is she?" Tegan asked.

"None of your business anymore now," Alicia teased as she ripped up the posters in her hand, "Oops! I slipped." Tegan squinted her eyes out of anger at Alicia's lack of respect.

"Who the heck does she think she is?" she thought. *"Destroying my property after all she's done?"* Tegan impulsively took a step forward. Alicia smirked further which incensed Tegan's already fraught nerves. Just as Tegan was about to do something stupid, the front door was opened and closed again. A blonde, slender woman walked through the hallway and into the living room to see Alicia and Tegan mere inches away from each other. Alicia spotted the blonde woman, went over to her and brought her into a passionate kiss. Tegan turned away, unwilling to witness the spectacle of her ex-girlfriend and lover kissing to inflame her pain. The blonde woman and Alicia broke away and faced Tegan who wouldn't look at them.

"See? She's mine, you idiot," Alicia taunted as she walked away into the bathroom. Tegan turned her back to the blonde woman, crossing her arms as she did so.

"Tegan, come on, don't be like this!" she pleaded.

"Felicity, you only broke up with me yesterday. I haven't even found a place to live yet! You can't just replace me that quickly," Tegan angrily pointed out as she faced her ex.

"You're staying with one of your colleagues, aren't you?" Felicity tried to reason.

"On her sofa! It's not like I can store a load of my things in her tiny living room," Tegan mentioned. "Can't you just wait until I've figured out what I'm going to do?"

"Alicia doesn't want to stay at her parents' place anymore. You can understand, surely?"

"Not really, no."

"Why don't you just go back to your Mum's or friends back in Colton City?"

"Oh, so I'm supposed to just what: leave my job, uproot my entire life, and move across the country to satisfy you and Alicia? For goodness sake Felicity: we were together for three years. Do I not mean anything to you anymore?" Tegan pleaded. A silence befell the former lovers as the sound of the toilet flushing was heard. Within moments, Alicia came back into the living room and put her arm around Felicity.

"I made up my mind," Felicity said with sudden firmness. "I'm with Alicia now and only her. You need to get yourself together." A sense of quiet the trio of women standing in front of each other as Tegan was unsure how to respond. Alicia and Felicity left the living room, shutting the door behind them as they went into the main bedroom. A single tear trickled down Tegan's face as she felt a mix of anger and sorrow but tried her best not to let it show too much for she still didn't want to give Alicia what Tegan felt she wanted.

"Fine," Tegan thought to herself. *"I know when I'm not wanted."*

A little while later into the day, Tegan turned up at the front door of her colleague's house holding the sports bag and one of the boxes from her flat. She knocked on the door and waited to be let in. A woman in hospital-branded scrubs answered the door.

"Tegan! Are you okay?"

"Hey Abigail," Tegan greeted her as she was let in. "Thanks again for letting me crash here."

"It's okay! You're welcome to stay until you've sorted what you're going to do," Abigail assured her. "I don't expect that to be quick but—"

"I already figured it out," Tegan interrupted as she placed her things by the cream sofa she'd slept on the night before in a determined manner. "If she wants me gone, then I guess I better go." Tegan grabbed her laptop, covered in polyamory and pansexual pride stickers, and turned it on. Abigail sat gently next to Tegan, concerned for what she might do.

"Tegan, don't rush into anything. You know you can stay as long as you need to," Abigail tried to reassure her. Tegan sighed, feeling a little self conscious that she'd appeared ungrateful.

"I need to move forward. They clearly are, so why shouldn't I?" Abigail went into the kitchen as Tegan logged into her laptop. She tapped her fingers impatiently on the laptop until her desktop was fully loaded. She went straight to her web browser, went to NHS jobs, and started browsing for midwifery vacancies. As she searched through the postings, Abigail came back to the living room with a cup of tea for Tegan. She placed it on the coffee table near Tegan's laptop.

"I've got to get the spare key cut. I won't be long," Abigail told Tegan, who didn't acknowledge her. Abigail left the room as Tegan stumbled upon a posting for a role that caught her eye. She read the posting: a full time midwife role at her hometown hospital of Colton City that paid more than she currently was getting. She read through the vacancy in full before scrolling back up to the top of the page where there was a "Apply for this job" button. She was about to click it but something stopped her.

"I think I need to think about it," Tegan thought. *"Colton City is a long way away. Am I really prepared to move back and start again? Are Alicia and Felicity really enough to make me move across the country? Wouldn't it be better to try and make new friends here? Would the Colton City lot want me around? Is this really a good idea?"* Tegan noticed the cup of tea and started to drink it as she contemplated what she was going to do. She nervously tapped her fingers on the cup of tea as she thought about her next move. Just as she was about to lose her nerve, a Messenger message appeared on her phone. She checked it: it was from Alicia. It was a picture of her and Felicity in bed together under the covers with the caption: 'Mine now'. This made up Tegan's mind: if she was unsure before, that evaporated with the reading of the message from Alicia. All the feelings of anger towards Alicia and Felicity came raging back to the surface: their audacity, their callousness, and their betrayal. She put the cup of tea down on the coffee table, went back to her laptop and the job posting she hesitated over before. Without another thought: she pressed the application button.

Return To The Hometown

♥

I t was 8:15pm on a chilly April Friday, and Tegan was in maternity scrubs changing in a dingy, claustrophobic hospital changing room. She got into a tasteful yet short purple dress and delicate pink kitten heels. She released her long, auburn hair from a restrictive ponytail and retrieved her large handbag and a hanger from her locker, closing it behind her.

"*Okay,*" she thought to herself. "*Let's do this.*" She draped the scrubs and hanger over her back. She held onto her handbag tight as she walked along the corridor. She confidently walked through the maternity ward and approached the cream-coloured reception area which was eerily empty. The woman looked around to see if there was anyone about however couldn't see anyone who'd be able to help. She sighed in an irritated manner as she looked at her smart watch: the time was now 8:20pm.

"*For goodness sake,*" she thought to herself. "*I'm so late.*" She looked around again, growing increasingly agitated.

"Tegan!" Abigail shouted. "I'll take those!" Tegan turned to face the voice. She half smiled out of politeness but didn't look her fully in the eye.

"Hi Abigail," Tegan responded awkwardly as she handed over the scrubs to Abigail.

"Good luck over at Colton City. It's a shame you couldn't stay here but I totally understand why you're moving." Abigail started.

"Yeah what a shame," Tegan lied with a fake smile on her face. Tegan turned to the doorway. An irritated Alicia was pacing outside with a couple of suitcases and a box in her hands. Alicia and Tegan made brief eye contact. Tegan felt a punch to the heart: she dreaded seeing her but wasn't surprised. She turned back to Abigail.

"I'm sorry but I need to go." Tegan quickly said as she left. A feeling of irritation and dread flooded over Tegan as she went towards Alicia. She didn't want to deal with this but she knew she must.

"I'm sorry I'm late Alicia," Tegan apologised. "I—"

"I don't care, Tegan. Just take your stuff. Felicity and I are late for our date because of you," Alicia barked at Tegan.

"More's the pity," Tegan muttered under her breath. Alicia chucked Tegan's box at her, who just about caught it before it hit the floor. Tegan felt stupid for feeling it, but she still felt betrayed by the former girlfriend who left her for a monogamous woman and didn't have the guts to face her a final time.

"Seriously, can you ever be on time for anything?" Alicia snidely remarked. This pissed Tegan off, but she wanted to be careful not to give Alicia what Tegan felt she wanted: anger.

"Should I have told the woman giving birth to hurry up because my ex-girlfriend's lover can't wait twenty minutes?" Tegan remarked sarcastically. Another person with a half buzz cut approached Tegan and Alicia. They went to Tegan's side and held the handle of one of the suitcases. Tegan felt relieved to see them appear.

"Do you ever just think about how much of a butthole you are to my best friend or..." they asked smarmily. Tegan smiled whilst Alicia rolled her eyes. Alicia walked away, sighing in contempt as she walked into the distant darkness. Tegan faced the person and held her arms out for a hug. The person embraced her carefully, being sure not to squish the box she was holding.

"Thanks Nadia," Tegan greeted them.

Twenty minutes elapsed, and Nadia & Tegan were in a car together driving along the motorway. The motorway was surprisingly busy with cars racing to their destination. Nadia concentrated on the drive ahead, ensuring they drove safely whilst Tegan stimmed with her hands, rubbing her palms together in a soothing way. Nadia noticed this before turning their glance back on the road.

"How was work today?" Nadia asked.

"Busy," Tegan remarked as she concentrated on stimming. "Yours?"

"I only did a half day of teaching," Nadia explained.

"Why?" Tegan enquired absentmindedly. Nadia glanced at Tegan briefly, trying to gauge where their friend's mind was. A silence fell between them as Nadia continued to drive along.

"Does Alicia suddenly grow a rod up her arse or was she always like that?" Nadia asked. Tegan stopped stimming to laugh a little.

"Okay, you've got my attention!" Tegan said in jest.

"I'm being serious though," Nadia continued. "She steals your girlfriend, makes her go monogamous, and has the nerve to not only give you attitude, but she also nearly breaks your things."

"Felicity is the bigger coward for not facing me herself," Tegan remarked. She hesitated as the feelings of the past few months washed over her in a second. She almost choked up as she remembered the moment Felicity broke it off with her and everything in the run up: the lies, the secrecy, and the heartbreak.

"Do you want to talk about it?" Nadia asked her. Tegan shook her head, almost as if to shake away the feeling for now. Whilst she felt she could always rely on Nadia's blunt honesty for clarity, she didn't feel ready to disclose these feelings.

"It doesn't matter right now," Tegan rallied. "Hopefully that's the worst breakup I'm ever involved with."

It was midnight in the southern English city of Colton City, the bustling place of opportunities for all who seek it. Among the bustle of a city at nighttime, there was a quiet suburbia that was a deep sleeper in the dark hours. Nadia drove into the driveway of a semi-detached house. The house had a light on in the hallway that could be seen through the front door window. It was so quiet the only noise that could be heard was the car slowly crawling over crunchy leaves. As they parked in the parking space, put on the hand brake and took the key out of the ignition, Nadia turned to face Tegan.

"We're home!" Nadia exclaimed. Tegan faced Nadia with a relieved smile on her face.

"That's the best thing I've heard all day," Tegan rejoiced. "We better be quiet though: won't Magda be asleep?"

"She's too excited for your arrival to be asleep. Work be damned!" Nadia informed her. They both started unloading Tegan's belongings from the car, but Tegan took pause to stare up at the house. This was her new home: a chance to restart in her hometown. She felt a mixture of anticipation and fear.

"*How can I know this is going to go any better than where I was a mere few hours ago?*" She thought to herself. "*Can I really trust I've done the right thing by leaving my job and moving away?*" Nevertheless, she proceeded into the house with Nadia. As they took their shoes off, a mid-twenties blonde woman in a dressing gown and a nightie came in from the kitchen with a mug in each hand.

"Nadia! Tegan! I prepared some hot chocolate for you," Magda said with glee. They put down the things in the hallway. Nadia approached Magda and took one of the hot chocolate mugs. They went into the living room/dining area as Magda handed the other hot chocolate mug to Tegan.

"You and Nadia are already the best housemates," Tegan said to Magda. They went into the living room. Tegan sat on the sofa in between Nadia and Magda. The living room smelt of the rose incense sticks burning on the large sideboard. A tabby Maine coon cat was snoring peacefully on a cat bed by the television opposite the sofa.

Day One

♥

"Oedipus seems settled, Nadia," Tegan commented.

"We only moved in a week ago but he's a quick learner. If he knows he's being fed, he sticks around," Nadia replied.

"So, Tegan," Magda started. "How do you feel?" Tegan hesitated for a moment. She perceived an intense look of intrigue from both her friends as they both held their gaze at her, awaiting her answer. It put Tegan on edge: she didn't feel ready for a heart wrenching confessional just yet.

"I feel like this is the right move," Tegan replied. "Colton City Hospital is one of the better hospitals to work in. The Head of Midwifery seems nice so I should get on."

"That's not what I meant," Magda pushed back. Tegan fidgeted with her mug with some discomfort. She took a sip out of her hot chocolate. As she swallowed, her legs started to shake a little. She quickly stopped herself but still felt tense.

"I'm not sure Tegan is quite ready for that chat, Mags," Nadia suggested. Magda's face displayed a sense of guilt.

"I'm sorry Tegan. You're tired and it must still be a bit fresh," Magda apologised.

"It's okay. I understand you're curious. I just—" Tegan hesitated, trying to figure out the right way to explain to her friend how she felt. She felt self-conscious at being the centre of attention in this context.

"It's just been a hard few months," Tegan conceded. Oedipus stretched on his cat bed and started to wander around. Nadia put their hot chocolate down on the coffee table, went over to him, and picked him up. They turned to Magda and Tegan, holding the relaxed cat.

"Do you want to cuddle Oedipus? It's like cuddling a large teddy bear," Nadia offered. Tegan felt a little unsure but didn't want to be rude, so she nodded. Nadia carefully placed Oedipus on Tegan's lap. Tegan started stroking him as he loudly purred. She got out of him something she craved: a distraction. She could focus on stroking the cat and very little else. A small smile came across her face as she continued to channel her attention on Oedipus, who appreciated the attention himself. Eventually, he jumped off Tegan and wandered towards the living room/dining area door. Nadia opened the door and followed him to the conservatory.

"I think I just need a bit of sleep," Tegan said as she got up from the sofa. "It's been a long day and I still need to make the bed."

"I made your bed for you so you could go straight to bed," Magda informed her. Tegan smiled wearily.

"Thanks Mags. Goodnight." Tegan left the room with her mug of hot chocolate. She slowly made her way up the stairs. She got to her bedroom, which had a myriad of boxes and suitcases on the floor that had arrived a week before. Her bed was made with a teddy bear lying between the dark blue pillows and duvet. Tegan placed the mug on the bedside table and kicked off her shoes under her bed. She sat on the bed in contemplation. She still felt anxious over the events of the evening but didn't want to dwell too much on it. After a while, she lay back on the bed and started to fall asleep.

The following day at 4pm dawned on the residents of Colton City. Tegan was sitting in a busy cafe with a heavily pregnant, auburn-haired woman. The cafe was small with many paintings from local artists on the wall. The two were talking to each other as many others flooded into the cafe for their mid-afternoon caffeine hits.

"Thanks for meeting up with me, Sara."

"What are big sisters for?" Sara responded happily.

"I know but Mum made it sound like you had lots to do," Tegan said, uneasy.

"That's because Mum is dealing with teenage boy stuff. She's getting sick of the testosterone fuelled nonsense, so she has to focus on her impending grandchild instead," Sara pointed out.

"She also mentioned your blood pressure has been a bit all over the place: is your midwife happy with everything?" Tegan quizzed, anxious about her sister. Sara laughed.

"Don't go into work mode. Everything is okay with both of us," Sara tried to reassure her younger sister as she stroked her growing bump happily. Tegan tried to brush away her concerns by focusing on her sister's happiness.

"It's a bit adorable seeing you stroke your bump," Tegan commented.

"You'll be doing it too if you ever get pregnant," Sara replied. An awkward silence fell between the two as Tegan fidgeted, uncomfortable with what Sara said.

"How're you feeling about the break-up?" Sara asked kindly. Tegan sighed. This annoyed her but she didn't feel she could hide her feelings from her older sister.

"I think it would've been easier if I'd been able to get away faster after we broke up, but the NHS takes its sweet time with its background checks and all," Tegan complained. "Plus her new girlfriend is actually horrible."

"You're not just saying that?" Sara challenged.

"What do you expect me to say? She convinced my polyamorous girlfriend to go monogamous with her then proceeded to torment me about it. I'm not exactly going to like her all that much," Tegan explained.

"Fair enough. I just don't want you to wallow in bitter self-pity or anything," Sara said with some concern in her voice. Tegan appreciated the concern but still felt a little uncomfortable.

"I won't. I promise. Besides, I've moved away from her now: I want to move forward too," Tegan attempted to reassure her older sister who seemed somewhat convinced.

"That's the spirit," Sara proclaimed. "I'll bet there's a bunch of hot doctors to ogle at the hospital. I don't know if it's just my hormones but every other consultant I saw on your new ward made my heart flutter a little."

"I think that's just the hormones talking," Tegan brashly responded. "The consultants I've worked with before weren't much to write home about."

"You never know, Tegan. You may meet one of your true loves there," Sara suggested.

Three hours elapsed. Sara and Tegan walked slowly along Tegan's new street towards her semi-detached house. Tegan kept an eye on her. She couldn't help it: her brain went into midwife mode, looking out for any signs of trouble. Tegan took comfort in focussing on her sister in a more work-like capacity. She knew how to be a midwife, she knew what to do in case of an emergency, and she knew how to remain calm and collected.

"Don't analyse me like that, Tegan," Sara asked politely. "You'll make me paranoid."

"Sorry. It's part midwife brain, part autism brain," Tegan apologised. The pair reached a bench. Sara sat herself carefully down on it. She faced away from her home which was opposite the bench and focussed her attention on Sara again, this time in a more sisterly capacity.

"At least this is a quiet neighbourhood. You'll at least get a good night's sleep if Magda and Nadia aren't too loud," Sara remarked. This snapped Tegan out of what was left of her work mode mentality long enough to engage in another form of conversation.

"Mags and Nadia aren't party animals who pull all-nighters. We all have jobs and such," Tegan remarked.

"I wouldn't be so sure about that," Sara hinted.

Surprise!

♥

Tegan was confused by what Sara would have meant: she knew her friends better than Sara did so why would she say that? She decided not to push it any further though, not wishing to start some silly argument with her. Sara received a text but hid it from Tegan.

"Who was that?" Tegan asked, suspicious.

"Just my partner being my partner," Sara brushed Tegan off. "Could I have a glass of water at your place?" Tegan, still a little suspicious, helped her sister up from the bench. They walked slowly together to Tegan's house. She opened the front door and went into the hallway followed by her sister. It was eerily quiet with the exception of a meowing Oedipus in the living room.

"That's odd," Tegan muttered to herself. She went to the living room and was met with:

"SURPRISE!" A raucous noise bellowed from the crowd of old friends that had formed in Tegan's living room/dining area. She was taken aback whilst Sara stood beside her with a smile on her face. Tegan was not used to being the centre of attention and she had to compose herself from the surprise as she faced her sister.

"You knew about this," Tegan accused her sister light-heartedly.

"Why do you think I insisted on going out for the afternoon?" Sara cheekily replied. Tegan hugged Sara, partially out of gratitude but also as a need to decompress from the adrenaline rush. Magda and Nadia emerged from the back of the small crowd as Tegan let go of Sara.

"We wanted to throw you a proper 'Welcome Home' party," Magda informed Tegan.

"You are both crafty buggers," Tegan said. She smiled as she adjusted to the situation at hand. She felt grateful to her friends and sister for putting in such an effort to welcome her home.

"And now my work is done, I better go home," Sara began. The crowd started socialising amongst themselves as Tegan faced her sister.

"Thanks for being so sneaky," Tegan thanked her sister as she hugged her again.

"You're welcome. Try not to get a hangover ahead of tomorrow's shift," Sara warned.

"Yes, Mother," Tegan responded sarcastically. Whilst she pretended as if Sara was a pain in the moment, she appreciated her care for her. With that, Sara took her leave. Tegan went to the kitchen to see two women she recognised making out with each other. Once she realised who it was, she folded her arms in a playful manner, keen to make a remark.

"Ladies, how about leaving the eroticism for later when we're all drunk?" Tegan teased. The two women stopped and faced her sheepishly.

"I *was* going to prepare you a 'Welcome Home' cocktail, but Jools distracted me," The first woman said pointedly.

"Georgia, if you can't control yourself long enough to make one singular cocktail you have bigger issues at hand," Jools argued.

"Do I need to separate you already?" Tegan further teased them. Jools and Georgia laughed slightly at her.

"We missed you, Tigs," Georgia remarked.

"I missed you two too," Tegan replied, appreciating the sentiment. "Now, that cocktail sounds fantastic. I could use a bit of alcohol to decompress with."

"I'll leave you two to it," Jools said happily as she left Georgia and Tegan. Georgia gathered ingredients from the bottles on the kitchen counter then got ice out of the freezer.

"I'm going to make your favourite: Long Island Iced Tea minus tequila," Georgia told Tegan as she put the ice bag on the counter. "Where do your large bowls live?"

"Oh, there should be one in one of the cupboards beneath the counter," Tegan explained. As she was about to come and help, she heard a knock on the front door. Her face crinkled with bewilderment.

"I thought everyone was already here?" Tegan thought to herself as she walked to the front door. She opened the door to a tall, blonde man wearing a tight t-shirt and jeans. They locked eyes and they looked at each other for what felt like forever. She felt a mix of excitement and joy at seeing him.

"Lloyd Thomas, is that you?" Tegan spluttered out of amazement.

"Hello Tegan," Lloyd greeted with a charming smile on his face.

"Come in," Tegan said as she stepped back. Lloyd stepped into the hallway and shut the door behind him, looking behind him as he did with a sense of agitation. Tegan noticed and became a little concerned.

"Everything okay?" Tegan asked innocently. Lloyd turned back to face Tegan in a more relaxed manner.

"It's fine. How're you?" Lloyd asked, focusing his attention on Tegan.

"Yeah, I'm good," Tegan started hesitantly. "Sorry I'm just shocked to see you."

"Why?"

"Well—" Tegan started, fidgeting with her dress.

"Tigs! Your drink is ready!" Georgia shouted out from the kitchen. Before Tegan knew it, Georgia came into the hallway, holding a huge pitcher of a brown coloured cocktail. Tegan's eyes widened as she stopped fidgeting.

"Is that all for me?" Tegan enquired jokingly.

"It's your party, love. Drunkenness is the order of the day!" Georgia exclaimed. She went into the living room and closed the door behind her.

It was 9pm and the party was in full swing with music, drinks and chatter. All the party goers were in little groups chatting away and drinking together. Tegan came through the living room with a drink in her hand. She wasn't sure which bundle of folks to go to to talk with whilst everyone failed to notice she was in the room. She spotted Lloyd with another party goer, chatting away. Her heart fluttered a little as she saw him.

"*Old feelings die hard, clearly,*" she thought to herself as she started to approach him, "*At least I'm not feeling crappy anymore.*"

"So how are you these days? I only seem to see you when Gabriella posts about you," the party goer asked. Tegan felt a pang of nostalgic pain ripple go through her heart at the mention of that woman.

"Yeah you know me: I like to keep myself to myself on social media," Lloyd answered.

"How are you two anyway? Do I hear wedding bells at last?" the party goer teased. Lloyd shuffled uncomfortably as he spotted Tegan come to them. The party goer finished their drink and spotted Tegan.

"Hey Tegan! I'm going to get another drink," the party goer said as they walked away to the kitchen. Tegan took a sip of her drink as Lloyd smiled at her.

"What drink have you got there?" Lloyd asked Tegan.

"Oh, just a mimosa. I didn't want to get sloppy drunk too quickly especially after that large bowl of cocktail Georgia prepared for me," Tegan explained.

"I'm sure you're not a sloppy drunk. You're probably more of a fun drunk," Lloyd complimented her.

"How can you know? You've never seen me drunk," Tegan noticed.

"Maybe I should stick around and find out," Lloyd teased as he kept his eye on her. Tegan blushed and took a sip of her drink. She wished more than anything she'd stop blushing lest she look too obvious.

"Speaking of drunks; do you remember the time when Mr Harvey got wicked drunk ahead of the drama production of Romeo and Juliet?" Tegan reminisced.

"Oh wow that takes me back." Lloyd laughed. "I distinctly remember him heckling poor Romeo when he fumbled his lines."

"Gabriella just wouldn't stop preening herself whilst Romeo struggled." Tegan giggled. "I felt bad enough for him to perform opposite her."

"Yeah," Lloyd said uncomfortably. Tegan felt a pang of regret for bad mouthing Lloyd's girlfriend despite how she may feel about her. She suddenly drank all of her drink very quickly.

"Oh look at that. Excuse me while I get another drink," Tegan quickly explained as she made a beeline for the exit, leaving Lloyd on his own.

Burn Down The Disco

♥

A moment later, Tegan went back into the living room with another drink in her hand. The party goers, including Nadia, were surrounding Lloyd as he played a video of a gig on his phone. She was intrigued by the music coming out of the phone, enjoying the indie rock feel she got. Tegan approached cautiously as people moved for her to get to Lloyd, who looked up from his phone to see her.

"Who's playing? They sound good!" Tegan asked innocently.

"Me with my new band 'Burn Down The Disco'," Lloyd answered. "We played at The Purifier a couple of weeks ago." Tegan turned to look at the screen of the phone, standing rather close to Lloyd. Without her noticing, he turned to face her in a contemplative mood. He placed his arm around her as she watched. In an instant, Tegan felt a surge of excitement flow through her. She looked at him whilst he was focussed on his screen and became acutely aware of how close she was to him. Her heart raced a little but she was wary to read too much into it. Nadia seemed to notice their closeness but remained silent.

"Wait, wasn't your band called 'The Disease' during school?" Tegan remembered suddenly. The response from the party goers was of awkward grimaces as Lloyd turned off the music. The party goers dispersed to other areas of the room except for Nadia who went to get another drink. Lloyd took his arm away from Tegan.

"What?" Tegan asked.

"After our bassist got discovered by a bigger band during university, he and Gabriella had an affair," Lloyd confessed. Tegan's eyes widened both for not knowing this information but also out of empathy for Lloyd.

"Sorry."

"It's not your fault, you didn't know. You were away for university. I don't expect you to be vigilant for hometown gossip." Nadia came back into the room with another drink.

"So why stay with her?" Nadia asked bluntly. Tegan nudged them more violently than intended, causing them to spill their drink slightly. Lloyd looked as if he was thinking about the question posed to him. At that moment, a call came up on his phone: it was coming from a contact known as 'Baby' with heart emojis next to it.

"Excuse me," Lloyd said as he walked out of the room. Nadia and Tegan turned to face each other uncomfortably.

"Nadia!" Tegan whispered.

"Hey, I'm not the one who's staying with a horrible person for goodness knows why!" Nadia defended themself. They sipped their drink as Tegan looked to where Lloyd had left. He stood in the hallway, looking agitated as he spoke to the person on the phone. Tegan felt bad but her gut instinct told her not to go to him and to continue to party with everyone else.

10pm came and went. The party in Tegan's house had quietened down a little. There were a number of people still present, primarily in the living room/dining area, but in a more drunk manner. Magda, Jools, Georgia, Nadia and Tegan were chatting with each other in a squiffy manner towards the middle of the room. They were all holding cocktails in their hands. Jools and Georgia had their arms linked together.

"Tegan, now you're properly back in Colton City, you must come to the post-renovation party at the Shaky Martini next month," Georgia told her excitedly.

"I will. Let me know the date and I'll be there," Tegan agreed keenly. Georgia started to discuss the renovation of The Shaky Martini but Tegan was barely paying attention. She looked over at Lloyd who was chatting to another party goer. Her look was wistful, fuelled by the nostalgia of an old crush. Georgia, Jools, Nadia and Magda noticed.

"Hey girl, still got a bit of a flame for the old crush?" Magda teased Tegan.

"Shut up, Mags," Tegan retorted, desperately hoping he didn't notice her look or Magda's remark. She uncomfortably took a sip of her drink.

"Isn't he still with that woman you all told me about?" Jools asked politely.

"Yeah. There would've been a social media meltdown if they weren't," Georgia speculated dryly.

"Does she even know he's here? I know she gets apoplectic if he's doing something she doesn't like," Nadia asked.

"That's a very kind way of saying it," Tegan remarked. "She's not remembered for keeping particularly calm."

"She was such a cow at school. I still remember seeing her at university losing her marbles because they didn't have skimmed milk at the campus coffee place," Magda bleakly reminisced.

"Bloody hell. What does he see in her?" Jools asked.

"Pretty people gravitate towards pretty people?" Georgia theorised simplistically. At that moment, Lloyd started coming over to the quintet. Tegan's heart raced, not knowing what might happen.

"Folks, he's coming. Keep it down," Tegan whispered. The five turned to face Lloyd, trying to pretend as if they hadn't been discussing him behind his back.

"Tegan, do you still have any beer in the fridge?" Lloyd asked.

"Yeah we should have some. Want me to get it for you?" Tegan offered.

"I can get it, thanks," Lloyd declined. He walked into the kitchen. Magda nudged Tegan cheekily.

"Tegan, go after him. He clearly wants to talk to you," Magda encouraged her. Tegan became uncomfortable, fiddling with her straw.

"I just got out of a long-term relationship and he's in a monogamous relationship—" Tegan began.

"I'm not saying you should jump him. Chat. Catch up," Magda interrupted. She finished the rest of her drink quickly. "Whilst you're at it, get me another drink?" Tegan rolled her eyes at Magda's obviousness, feeling as if she had an ulterior motive. Tegan felt as if she was back at school: being teased by her friends whilst looking on at her crush with another woman. Regardless, she went into the kitchen to see Lloyd with an open beer in his hand. She stopped dead in her tracks, looking at Lloyd, and tried to maintain her composure.

"Everything okay?" Tegan asked.

"It's fine," Lloyd brushed off coolly. "Are you okay?"

"Yeah, fine," Tegan quickly answered. An awkward silence fell between the pair as Tegan started to pour herself a drink.

"Are you glad to be back in Colton City after all these years?" Lloyd asked.

"Yeah. All my friends and family are here so it makes sense." Tegan shrugged as she turned to face him again, holding her drink. Lloyd stepped slightly closer to Tegan.

"Didn't you make any friends at university?" Lloyd asked inquisitively. Tegan wasn't sure what his motive was but was too tipsy to give it much thought.

"I did but she became my ex-girlfriend," Tegan said with a twinge of bitterness. "Suddenly non-monogamy wasn't okay anymore."

"Non-monogamy isn't for everyone," Lloyd tried to justify.

"It definitely wasn't for the woman she ran off with," Tegan remarked, irritated. Lloyd placed his hand on Tegan's arm. Just the slightest touch, along with her drunkenness, made Tegan's heart race. She didn't show her feelings at that moment; after all she'd intended to just chat to him, not jump his bones in the kitchen.

A Forbidden Kiss

♥

"Are you sure Gabriella won't kill you for that?" Tegan said with concern. Lloyd took his hand away and took a sip of his beer. Tegan started to regret her comment; deep down, she didn't want him to stop touching her but she knew the consequences could be bad for both of them.

"I'm sorry. I—" Tegan started, trying to salvage the situation.

"No, you're right," Lloyd interrupted with a sigh. "She doesn't even know I'm here. She thinks I'm at the pub with my Dad." Tegan found that somewhat suspicious, however it didn't surprise her.

"Why do you stay with her if you're actively lying to her about your whereabouts?" Tegan asked bluntly. Lloyd hesitated and looked down. He placed his beer on the kitchen countertop.

"My ex-girlfriend did the same thing to me, and it sucked. You should be honest with Gabriella no matter how much of a bitch she is," Tegan blurted out.

"I don't even know if I want to be with her anymore," Lloyd admitted. He looked at Tegan, pained. They were so close one could pull the other into a kiss at any moment but Tegan resisted the temptation. For her part, she didn't want to cause a mess no matter how sorely she wanted him at that moment.

"If you don't want to be with her, you need to break it off. You can't lie to her," Tegan softly explained to him. He stroked her cheek. Her heart fluttered as they remained close. Tegan wanted to make sure things remained platonic, but her alcohol-induced haze was excited at their close proximity.

"You're still the great girl I knew at school," Lloyd told her. She smiled at him. Lloyd grasped Tegan and kissed her. She kissed him back, separated from the sober thoughts that would've stopped her. Tegan's excitement grew as the kissing turned increasingly passionate. Tegan's arms were around Lloyd's neck as she was on her tiptoes to reach him. Comprehensive thoughts seem to elude Tegan's head as they continued to snog each other. As their make-out session started to take on a whole new zenith, a loud smashing sound could be heard from the living room. This caused them to suddenly break apart: The reality of what they had done sunk in. Lloyd tried to hold Tegan again, but she backed away, scared of the impulse that led her down this path.

"You're with someone else monogamously. I can't be a part of that mess."

"But—" Lloyd started.

"Anything you might say now, you may come to regret in the morning," Tegan interceded firmly. Lloyd grabbed his beer and left the room. Tegan was in a quandary; she wanted Lloyd, but she didn't want to be a side piece. She didn't want to be secondary to another woman, especially one who was so awful at school. After a moment, she resolved to think of it no more. She gathered her courage, grabbed her drink from the counter top, and went back into the living room. She saw Magda and Nadia on the floor, drunkenly tidying up some glass. Tegan relished the distraction, so she rushed into the kitchen again, grabbed a dustpan & brush from a cupboard and rushed back into the living room. When she came back, the drunken crowd cheered.

"This might be a safer way to go, folks," Tegan suggested coolly as she crouched down on the floor. She swept up the broken glass. Nadia and Magda placed the shards in their hands in the dustpan. Once she was finished, Tegan went straight back to the kitchen to dispose of the glass shards. As she went back into the hallway, she saw Lloyd grab his jacket and leave the house. Tegan felt a pang of guilt and shame over what she had done but she couldn't help but want to run after him. She stared at the door, hoping he would return. After a while, a drunken Georgia and Jools came through the hallway, breaking Tegan's reverie.

"We're off, Tegan. We need to get my daughter back at a reasonable-ish hour," Jools explained to Tegan.

"Okay. Get home safely?" Tegan requested.

"We'll be okay, Tigs. Don't sweat it," Georgia drunkenly tried to assure her friend. Tegan giggled a little whilst Jools and Georgia stumbled to the door and made their way out. Tegan sighed as they shut the door.

She still felt the surging guilt almost consume her, but she didn't want to ruin the party atmosphere by breaking down or telling anyone. She composed herself and went back into the living room, where she found Nadia and Magda playing a card game called Piss'd with the remaining party guests.

"*They look so happy,*" Tegan mused in her head. She quietly closed the door, unnoticed. A feeling of tension and guilt gripped her heart. She sat on the stairs, placing a hand over her heart to feel its rapid heartbeat whilst the other gripped the stair she sat on. Her legs started to shake up and down. She started trying to breathe as calmly as she could to try and bring herself back down to Earth from her anxiety-riddled height.

"*Oh God! Oh God! Oh God! Gabriella is borderline psychotic and I kissed her boyfriend. What is he going to do? What is she going to do? What am I going to do?*" Tegan panicked in her mind, spiralling into an incredibly anxious mess. Realising she might completely lose the plot if she didn't calm down, she started to count her breaths in her head so as not to be overheard. As she continued to count one, two, three, four then one, two, three, four again and again, she began to calm down. Her legs eventually stopped shaking and she relaxed the hand that was on the stair. After she assured herself she was calm enough, she went up the stairs to her bedroom.

Tegan's phone alarm blasted around her bedroom as it hit 9am. She turned off the alarm quickly so the sound would stop. She got up feeling groggy, but relieved not to be hungover. She slowly got out of bed and grabbed the glass of water from her bedside table. She took a sip of her water. The events of the night before with Lloyd echoed in her head:

"*Why did he kiss me? Is this some sort of game? Why do I still fancy him after all this time? Why did I kiss him back?*" She was desperate to try and think about anything else without spiralling into another anxiety attack. She looked at the mostly packed boxes and suitcases. She tapped her glass in anxiety, trying to figure out what she was going to do.

"*Where did I place my new uniform?*" she thought to herself. The realisation soon kicked in: she was going to have to go through every suitcase and box until she found it. This was both good and bad: bad because she didn't want to be late because she couldn't find her uniform, yet it was good because it gave her something else to focus on. She decided to go through every suitcase until she found what she was looking for. She went to a large, hard, orange suitcase and opened it. The clothes inside smelt of her previous home with Felicity. A pang of sadness shot through Tegan as she smelt that scent again: a part of her longed for the seemingly uncomplicated relationship she had with her now-ex.

"I miss what I thought there was; simplicity," she thought sadly to herself. She shook her head. Nothing she felt would change the facts of the matter at hand. She resolved to move forward. She went through all the clothes in that suitcase but couldn't find what she was looking for. She put all the clothes back in the orange suitcase, zipped it up and placed it on her bed. She went for the next one; an older pink & blue with the progressive pride sticker on it. She placed it on the floor, opened it and immediately found her uniform; a Stuart blue tunic with white piping, and a pair of blue trousers and wipeable shoes. The relief flooded through her as she held the tunic in her hands.

"Thank goodness! It's time to get ready for work and stop thinking about exes or people I shouldn't kiss." She promptly got out of her pyjamas and got into her work uniform, putting deodorant on her armpits in between clothing. Feeling fresh and clean made Tegan feel a little better within herself.

The Meet Cute

♥

A few minutes later, Tegan came down the stairs and went into the kitchen. She came across Nadia in their pyjamas, tidying up the glasses quietly.

"Do you want some help?" Tegan offered. Nadia faced Tegan.

"No thanks," Nadia declined. "You look great in your uniform."

"Thanks," Tegan replied. As she was about to go to the kettle to make a cup of tea, she heard a knock at the door. She headed towards the hallway via the living room, but Magda answered the door first.

"Hi Magda," a male voice greeted. "Is Tegan home?" Tegan recognised that voice; it was Lloyd. Her anxiety went into near overdrive as she stepped away from the door before she could be spotted. Magda, unaware of Tegan's whereabouts, turned to face the stairs.

"Tegan!" Magda yelled out. Tegan went back into the kitchen, returning to a confused Nadia. Nadia was about to say something when Tegan gestured at them to be quiet. Nadia was confused by what was going on but remained quiet.

"Tegan?" Magda yelled again from the hallway. Tegan and Nadia didn't make a sound as they waited. Nadia placed glasses that were in their hand silently on the counter.

"I'm sorry Lloyd," Magda said to him. "She's either not in or still asleep."

"Could you tell her I stopped by?" Lloyd requested keenly.

"Sure," Magda agreed.

"Okay. Thanks," Lloyd said as he walked away. Magda shut the front door. She turned to the living room to see Tegan in the doorway, looking apprehensive.

"Tegan! You just missed—" Magda started.

"I know," Tegan interrupted. Magda looked at Tegan, confused. Tegan approached Magda, followed by Nadia who was now carrying a rubbish bag.

"What's going on?" Magda asked in a suspicious manner. Tegan sighed, fidgeted with her tunic, and faced the others. She didn't want to tell them but felt she was unable to lie to them any longer.

"Lloyd and I kissed last night," Tegan confided in her friends.

"That's the least surprising and yet the most surprising development," Nadia surmised. Tegan looked at them, perplexed.

"It's not surprising because you two fancied each other in sixth form. It is surprising because I thought you were not into monogamous people," Nadia explained themself.

"That makes a lot of sense." Magda shrugged in agreement. "But you can't do that again whilst he's in a monogamous relationship with Ms Bunny Boiler."

"Nothing good can come of this. This is the same woman who set that girl's—" Nadia warned. Tegan couldn't help but feel bombarded and a bit annoyed at being told the obvious but appreciated their concern.

"I know. You're both right. I just wish it wasn't like this. I don't need this," Tegan interrupted Nadia. Magda went to give her a hug when Tegan looked at her mobile phone: the time was now 9:20am.

"Oh shit," Tegan uttered. "I've got the leave before 10am for work. I was going to try and do some unpacking before I left."

"Is there anything we can do to help?" Magda offered.

"Maybe let Jools and Georgia know what's going on? I don't want any of us to keep secrets from two of our best friends," Tegan asked. Nadia and Magda nodded in agreement, sticking with their best friend's resolve.

It was 3pm on a hectic day of work and Tegan was sitting alone in the staff room preparing a Pot Noodle to eat. The staff room smelt of old coffee and a previous microwaved fish curry meal. It was quite a small room and would feel claustrophobic with a crowd inside. Tegan wasn't thinking about the night before anymore: she was very much focussed on her first day at work which made her feel happier in herself.

"Let's not think about attractive people today. Let's focus on getting through the work day!" As the kettle came to boil, the door opened. She turned and faced the man who entered: a well-chiselled, dark haired tall man in a slightly too tight blue shirt and black trousers. Tegan was struck at how attractive he was to her. It was as if a lightning strike of attraction hit her hard as her heart raced slightly. Her resolve not to think about attractive people went out the window. Nevertheless, she quickly composed herself and went back to her Pot Noodle.

"Have we met?" the man asked. His voice was smooth like caramel. It went through Tegan and almost made her melt. She turned and faced him out of politeness.

"No. I'm new. I just—" Tegan started. At that moment a short, thin, middle aged woman in a midwife's uniform came into the staff room.

"Ah! I see you two have met!" she said happily.

"Actually, we were just introducing each other, Sinead," the man explained.

"I'm Tegan. I'm the new midwife."

"I'm Darcy, one of the trainee consultants. It's a pleasure to meet you," Darcy introduced himself with a half-smile. Tegan smiled back at him politely. She had to restrain herself from a big smile: she didn't want to come off as creepy or over-enthusiastic.

"I'm going to get lunch. It looks as if you're sorted, Tegan. I'll see you in half an hour," Sinead said right before she left the room. Tegan poured the boiling water into the Pot Noodle carefully to the fill level. She turned to see Darcy standing behind her.

"So, what brought you to Colton City hospital?" Darcy asked courteously. Tegan placed the lid over the pot noodle.

"I grew up here so once my ex and I broke up, it felt natural to come back," Tegan explained honestly, as if on autopilot. She turned back to face Darcy. "How about you?"

"I've always lived here," Darcy said, maintaining his cool composure. "I didn't want to move away when this is one of the better hospitals. Besides, I have a teenager to consider."

"Oh, you're a father?" Tegan asked, intrigued.

"No. She's my little sister," Darcy clarified. As Tegan was about to ask a follow-up question, they both heard a scream. They snapped into action, running to the scream. A heavily pregnant woman who was crying hysterically in the main waiting area. Sinead was standing nearby whilst a shocked receptionist stood behind the desk.

"Miss, can we help you?" Sinead tried in a kind tone.

"He won't leave her! He said he'd leave her for me and my baby!" the distressed woman screamed at Sinead.

"Look, why don't we go into another room and get you a glass of water?" Sinead offered, approaching her slowly.

"No! I don't want water! I want him and I want him now!" the woman screamed back, causing Sinead to step back. A security guard came through the main entrance door of the maternity department. The woman tried to call someone but when she couldn't get through, she threw the phone across the floor. It hit the floor hard, smashing into pieces as it did so. The security guard was about to take action when Darcy stepped forward. The woman crumbled to the floor and started to sob again. Darcy crouched on the floor opposite the woman, staying at her eye level.

We All Make Mistakes

♥

"**I** don't know why I listened." The woman sobbed. "He said he'd leave her."

"I'm sorry. That must be really difficult, especially when you're expecting," Darcy softly empathised with the woman. "If he can't get his act together long enough to support you both then he doesn't deserve either of you." The woman raised her head to face Darcy.

"You're not just saying that?" the woman asked.

"Of course not. You and your baby deserve nothing but the best and he clearly isn't that," Darcy soothed her. The woman started to get up but struggled so Darcy helped her up.

"Why don't we go into a calm room for a bit and—" Darcy began until she saw the woman's waters had broken. Darcy turned to face Sinead and Tegan who started to approach. Darcy then faced the woman who looked frightened.

"Okay, my colleagues and I are going to get you ready," Darcy assured her as they walked away from the waiting area into the ward.

9pm finally hit and Tegan was preparing to leave the hospital. She was in the staff room again, changing into her trainers. She felt exhausted from her shift; this was a much busier hospital than her previous workplace where she jumped right into helping women deliver their children whilst under supervision. Having said that, she was satisfied it had gone as well as it did. As she stood up, Darcy came through the door. He was now dressed in clean scrubs and non-slip shoes. In spite of his now clinical appearance, his dashing looks were still obvious to Tegan. For her, it was like being in the presence of a swoon-worthy literary character in real life.

"Darcy, isn't it?" Tegan asked politely, trying to strike a conversation.

"Yes," Darcy replied with a smile. "Well done for remembering my name on the first day."

"I haven't the best memory with names so if I forget it tomorrow, please don't take it personally," Tegan explained.

"I'm the same," Darcy told her. "Blame the neurodiverse brain."

"Me too!" Tegan said enthusiastically. A silence fell between the two where Tegan felt immediately self-conscious over her enthusiasm whilst Darcy smiled at her.

"Sorry, it's just I've never met a neurodivergent doctor before, and I got a bit excited," Tegan apologised. She fidgeted with her tunic uncomfortably in a stimming fashion. Darcy stepped a little closer to her. His hands were behind his back, stimming in a way she couldn't see.

"No need to apologise," Darcy assured her. "I have seldom met fellow neurodivergent colleagues, so I understand." Tegan smiled back at him, and they both stopped stimming. She felt more comfortable around him at that moment. She started to feel like a connection was forming between them.

"I was impressed with the way you dealt with the upset patient earlier," Tegan complimented Darcy.

"It was nothing," Darcy coolly replied.

"You were great."

"So were you. You were very gentle with her."

"It's what we're supposed to do. Besides, I've been screwed over by a partner before. I don't wish that on anyone," Tegan remarked sadly. She looked to the side briefly before facing Darcy again.

"We all mess up in monogamy."

"There's a mistake and then there's systemic manipulation," she said with a tilt of the head and a rise of one of her eyebrows.

"Touche. Maybe men are idiots," Darcy conceded with a knowing smile on his face.

"What do you mean 'maybe'?" Tegan remarked with a smile. Darcy laughed at her comment.

"Good point. I better get dressed and head home. Goodnight, Tegan."

"Goodnight." Tegan sat down as Darcy left the room. She felt a happiness she hadn't felt for a while; the ease of being around someone who seems to understand her in a near-instant, the flutter of being around someone attractive, and the feel of a fresh introduction to a new person. Whilst a part of her felt sad for the life she used to have, the prospect of moving on finally felt exciting for her. This was part of the fresh start she'd hoped for by moving back to her hometown for a new job. She felt at ease with the situation and hopeful for a blossoming friendship.

Lloyd walked along the streets of Colton City alone after a practice session with his band. He was contemplating what he needed to do in his head. His thoughts were swirling on his situation: should he stay with his long-term girlfriend Gabriella, or should he leave her in order to pursue Tegan? Was any of this the right thing to do? As he got stuck in his thoughts he encountered a happy couple talking and cuddling each other on a bench.

"*It's never organic like that with Gabriella,*" Lloyd thought to himself. "*It's always engineered for bloody Instagram.*"

He continued to walk home in his own mental quandary when he got a text. It was from Gabriella. It read: "Get yourself to me right now. We need to talk.*"* Lloyd's insides were filled with dread, knotted out of fear. He knew what a text without a kiss meant from her; he was in trouble. He started to rush along towards the high street to a fancy complex of flats. Georgian architecture was present on this high quality building with a distinct lantern frieze, an arrangement of cast metal balustrades, and balconies at every flat. Lloyd looked up towards a particular flat. He could see a figure staring back at him in underwear and a pink negligee.

"*There she is,*" he thought to himself unenthusiastically. She turned away from him and retreated into her flat. He sighed with a feeling of defeat. The silent interaction merely confirmed what he feared. He went to the flat complex entrance, punched the number for his girlfriend's flat and rang it. Without a word, the entrance door buzzed. Lloyd walked through to the lobby. He dawdled through the luxury balcony of flora and fauna to get to Gabriella's flat, prolonging the inevitable. He knocked tentatively at the door and the it opened slightly. He sighed, went through the door and shut it behind him.

"*Great. Drama time,*" Lloyd thought. There was no one in the hallway but a light was emanating from the bedroom. His heart raced out of anxiety over what might happen next. He walked slowly to the bedroom doorway where the woman in the pink negligee was sitting pouting on the bed, expecting him to start the conversation. Instead, he shuffled awkwardly into the bedroom. He stayed at a distance from her, afraid of getting close. She stood up and stepped towards him.

"What time do you call this?" the woman spat out.

"Gabriella, I came as fast as I could," Lloyd explained. A silence fell between them which pissed off Gabriella more.

"Do you have nothing to say?" Gabriella said venomously.

"What do you want me to say?" Lloyd asked, a little confused as to what she was specifically upset about.

"I was thinking something along the lines of 'I'm sorry, my love, for betraying you' or 'Please forgive me for going to that party behind your back.'" Gabriella said with increasing anger in her voice.

"What do you mean?" Lloyd said impulsively. Gabriella grabbed her phone from her bed and went right up to Lloyd's face. On the phone was a photo of Lloyd at Tegan's party with Tegan, Magda, Jools, Georgia & Nadia on it.

The Strike

♥

Gabriella shoved the phone in Lloyd's face. He put his head down, stood back a step and bit his lip, tense and scared.

"What part of 'No' do you not understand?" Gabriella yelled at him as she threw her phone back on her bed, enraged.

"You can't tell me what I can and can't do," Lloyd snapped. "I'm a grown man." This defiance seemed to shock and anger Gabriella further.

"You're my boyfriend and you'll do what you're told." Gabriella scowled at him. "Now get your apology done and come to bed." She moved back to the bed and sat in what she felt was a seductive manner. For the first time, he was astounded by what she was saying and doing. It was as if his brain had snapped out of a fog-like haze. He felt disgusted at the idea of doing anything she asked, especially something sexual after being yelled at like that.

"I'm not getting into bed with you," Lloyd said firmly. Gabriella looked at him, appalled. She got up from the bed and stood in front of him, angry.

"What is the meaning of this?" Gabriella glared quietly. This struck a note of fear in Lloyd, but he knew he had to stand strong.

"I'm not getting into bed with you," Lloyd repeated defiantly.

"And why not?" Gabriella asked indignantly.

"I can't go on with this." Lloyd turned away but Gabriella grabbed his arm. She forcibly and aggressively turned him back to her.

"Let go of me!" Lloyd tried to yank his arm back, but she dug her nails in, causing some pain.

"Why would you embarrass me?" Gabriella said through gritted teeth.

"I'm sorry. I'm—" Lloyd tried to soothe her.

"I told you not to go to that party and you did it anyway behind my back." Gabriella raised her voice as she barely contained her anger. She let go of Lloyd's arm which had deep, red nail marks in them. Lloyd was rattled. She'd hurt him before but not left such marks.

"I knew you'd end up shagging that fat whore Tegan," Gabriella growled.

"Nothing like that happened between Tegan and me. It was just—"

"Do you think I'm stupid? She has to ruin everything all these years later!" Gabriella interrupted with venom.

"Leave her out of it! If anyone is the cheat, it's you," Lloyd snapped impulsively. "Remind me; was it three or four men you shagged behind my back? They didn't even give you the reality TV stardom you're so desperate for." Gabriella slapped him hard across the cheek. He turned to face her when she scratched his cheek with her nails.

"Get out, scumbag!" Gabriella yelled.

"We're done," Lloyd replied defiantly as he walked away. He rushed out of the bedroom and out of the flat with Gabriella following him close behind.

"Don't walk away from me! Don't leave me! Get back here!" she screamed as he left the flat. Lloyd fled the flat, quickly closing the door behind him. He felt his heart pound almost out of his chest from the adrenaline rush. He could hardly form the thoughts in his head to truly understand how he was feeling: he just knew he had to keep moving to get home.

It was 10pm and Tegan was getting off the bus near her street. She was exhausted from her long shift and could barely move but was in a positive mood about her day. She grabbed her phone from her pocket and realised it was dead.

"I could've sworn I charged this before work," she thought to herself, perplexed. "It's fine, I'm near home. I'll charge it there." As she started to walk towards her street she saw Jools waiting for her, looking concerned.

"Jools! What's up?" Tegan asked her, confused and tired.

"We tried to call you, but it went straight to voicemail," Jools informed her. "You're late home."

"Yeah I got held back thanks to a dodgy delivery at work. I think my phone died, which is strange because I could've sworn I charged it before I went to work," Tegan explained. She started to walk with Jools back towards her house. She was glad to see Jools but confused as to why she was met at the bus stop by her.

"Why are you—"

"Whatever you do when you get home, don't go on social media right now," Jools interrupted.

"What's going on?" Tegan asked, concerned at her friend's warning. Jools thought about waiting until they were back at Tegan's place but ultimately decided she couldn't keep her friend hanging.

"Gabriella seems to have found out Lloyd was at our party," Jools started. "She's decided you have shagged him and has gone on the warpath on social media." Tegan stopped, briefly put her head down and took a deep breath as she raised her head again. The anxiety she felt in the morning and previous night over Lloyd not only flooded back into her brain but tripled. This was worse than what she feared would happen. Whilst she wasn't entirely surprised by the sequence of events, she couldn't help but feel some of the old high school angst come back into her head. Jools stood next to her and placed an arm around her.

"Why does this feel like a high school drama all over again?" Tegan said in as measured a tone as possible. She didn't want to let on the extent of her feelings to Jools in the middle of the street.

"That was my first thought," Jools agreed.

"All I did was kiss him when he kissed me first," Tegan complained. "I swear we didn't do anything else."

"I believe you, Tegan," Jools assured her. Tegan felt a little better in the knowledge her friend believed her, but it barely compared to the negative feelings swirling her brain.

"Thanks Jools. I guess my phone died because of notifications set off by her crusade," Tegan surmised.

"Almost certainly," Jools agreed. "Let's get you home so we can sift through everything together." Tegan nodded. Jools removed her arm from Tegan, and they resumed their journey back to Tegan's house.

Lloyd was walking towards a semi-detached house that had a hallway light on. The semi-detached house was tall with a smoothly tiled driveway and a strong, wooden front door. As Lloyd walked up the driveway towards the entrance to the house, he noticed Georgia waiting for him outside. She was underneath the doorstep light, sitting on the step looking angry. Lloyd sighed, anticipating an epic argument between himself and Georgia.

"Lloyd!" Georgia greeted him in an angry tone. Lloyd stepped closer to the light where Georgia was able to see the bruise and scratches on his face. This softened Georgia's angry resolve.

"Jesus, what happened to you?" Georgia asked, appearing to be somewhat concerned.

"Gabriella. She decided to use her hand to get her anger across," Lloyd told her as he took a step back. "Why are you outside my Dad's house?"

"I needed to talk to you," Georgia answered as she crossed her arms. "What exactly did you say to Gabriella?"

It Started With A Post

♥

"She decided that Tegan and I slept together. I didn't tell her anything—she just seemed to decide on it and stick to the narrative in her head," Lloyd truthfully explained.

"So why did she post a video all over social media threatening to expose Tegan's nudes from your phone in retribution for stealing you from her?" Georgia interrogated him. Lloyd looked at her, confused and irritated.

"Okay, I only kissed Tegan. I've never seen her naked, let alone received a nude from her," Lloyd defended himself. "I don't even know if Tegan even does that." There was a tense moment between the pair where Lloyd could sense the contemplation going around Georgia's head. He was anxious over what might come out of her mouth next. She uncrossed her arms and placed them on her hips.

"I really want to be much angrier with you," Georgia admitted. "I remember what Gabriella was like at school, so this doesn't surprise me much."

"I broke up with Gabriella, for what it's worth," Lloyd told Georgia, matter of factly.

"Wow. How's that shiny new backbone of yours?" Georgia complimented him as her hands left her hips.

"It's nice, thanks," Lloyd said, smiling genuinely about the kindness Georgia just showed him.

"I feel awful for Tegan. She's had a long day delivering newborns only to come home to bollocks like this," Georgia lamented. Lloyd's smile turned upside down, realising how Tegan must be feeling about being dragged into the middle of a relationship drama she didn't start.

"I didn't mean for any of this to happen. She doesn't deserve any of this," Lloyd said in a regretful tone.

"You're right, she doesn't." Georgia started to leave but was stopped by Lloyd as he stepped in front of her.

"What should I do?" Lloyd asked, desperate to try and help. Georgia appeared to hesitate for a moment, briefly unsure how to handle the situation.

Jools and Tegan came through Tegan's front door into the hallway. As they were taking their shoes off, Magda came in from the living room.

"You two better come through," Magda said as she went back into the living room. Tegan and Jools followed her in. Tegan's nervousness increased at Magda's tone. A part of her didn't want to know what was being said online. She wanted to hide in her room and pretend it wasn't happening, but she knew she couldn't do that. Nadia made space for Tegan and Jools to sit on the sofa with them. Magda sat on a chair next to the sofa and handed Tegan a charger cable and portable charger.

"You really need to get one of these," Magda told Tegan as she handed them to her. "They're useful in an emergency i.e. if your sister goes into labour early."

"Thanks," Tegan said as she connected her phone to the charger. "I'll order one later."

"Whilst we're waiting for your phone to come back to life, do you want us to show you what's been posted? You can wait for your phone to load if you want but either way you should be prepared; it's not pretty," Nadia asked. Tegan looked around the room at her expectant friends, waiting for a response. She was exhausted: she didn't want to make decisions like this but there was no escape.

"Yeah. I've got to look at it eventually," Tegan said, resigned to her fate.

"I've taken screen grabs of everything on her Instagram account so just go to the photos app," Nadia informed her. Tegan held the phone in her hand and was struck again with dread. She did as she was told and scrolled through the screen grabs from the beginning. It started with a post from Gabriella's Instagram post shared to thousands of followers that slandered Tegan's character as a bully who stole away her 'precious' boyfriend Lloyd. There were multiple screen grabs of people supporting Gabriella blindly and making rude comments about Tegan without an ounce of consideration for the truth of the matter. Among the comments, there were only a mere few that suggested Lloyd was the one in the wrong: the rest were attacking Tegan with vigour. Tegan gave the phone back to Nadia, feeling deflated and demoralised by the things being said about her.

"I should've seen this coming." Tegan sighed.

"No. You don't deserve any of this," Magda tried to reassure her empathetically.

"Don't I? I let him kiss me," Tegan pointed out.

"That doesn't matter. You were the one who stopped it from going further, right?" Jools asked.

"Yeah," Tegan answered. "But—"

"No buts. You wouldn't say the same thing about us so why would you say it about yourself?" Magda reasoned with her. Tegan shot a small smile at her. At that moment, Tegan's phone came to life and vibrated with messages. Tegan picked it up and breathed in, preparing herself mentally for an onslaught.

"I guess I should check my requested messages on Instagram," Tegan said dejectedly. She went to Instagram and checked; the amount of them filled her with dread.

"Let's start from the beginning," Tegan said sarcastically. "'Hey slut, how about getting your own boyfriend?' Well, that one was mild but I'm sure it'll get worse." The other three stared at each other before looking back at Tegan. Tegan moved on to the next message with further unease.

"Here's another: 'I hope you're proud of yourself, you rancid whore.' Rancid: That's almost original." Tegan handed her phone to Magda as she stood up. Magda locked the phone as Tegan started pacing up and down the living room whilst rubbing her hands together, trying to relieve some tension within herself. The other three locked their attention on her.

"Tegan?" Jools asked.

"Sometimes pacing helps me calm down. It's almost an all body stim," Tegan explained.

"Okay then," Jools accepted.

"It's a good thing you haven't publicly listed where you currently work anywhere," Nadia remarked.

"Yes but everyone at that party knows what I do and where I now work. It's only a matter of time before Gabriella finds out," Tegan pointed out bluntly.

"Surely she wouldn't make it physical, would she?" Jools asked innocently.

"She got suspended from university for beating up a girl who she thought tried to flirt with Lloyd," Nadia explained to Jools.

"I would almost suggest getting rid of social media but honestly, I doubt that'll stop her. She seems determined to come after you," Magda commented. A knock on the door was heard which spooked everyone in the living room. It was enough to make Tegan stop moving.

"It's probably just Georgia. I'll get it," Jools reassured the others. She got up from the sofa and went into the hallway. Whilst Jools was gone, the other three could hear what was going on. They heard the door open and close again. The wait felt a lot longer for Tegan than it actually was. Every possible scenario she could think of raced through her head.

"*What is Gabriella going to do next? Is she going to come after me at home? What did Lloyd tell her? Where's Georgia?*" she thought to herself as she began to pace the room again.

"We've got you, love," Magda tried to reassure her anxious friend. Tegan shot a brief smile before resuming her pacing. Jools came back into the living room with Georgia in tow, which caused Tegan to stop pacing.

"Tegan, Lloyd's in the hallway. I think he just wants to talk to you. If you're not interested, I'll immediately kick him back to the curb. What do you want to do?" Georgia explained. Tegan's heart felt consumed by emotion. She was keen to hear him out and figure out a plausible way to deal with this mess, but her head told her to try to remain calm. She tried to make herself calm on the outside, as if she could fool people into thinking she has everything under control.

I Can't Let You Hurt Me

♥

"I don't know about this," Nadia protested. "Hasn't he done enough?"

"This isn't our decision, Nadia," Magda argued. "It's Tegan's and Tegan's alone. What do you want to do?" Everyone in the room faced Tegan who was internally nervous but trying to give an air of feeling sure.

"Okay," Tegan decided. "I'll hear him out."

"Come in, Lloyd," Georgia encouraged him. Lloyd sheepishly entered the room to the skeptical crowd around him. Tegan suddenly became very concerned at the state of Lloyd's face which was particularly pinkish-red.

"What happened to your cheek?" Tegan asked in concern.

"Gabriella got me a couple of times," Lloyd answered evasively. Tegan became concerned about how red his face was. It seemed redder than it should be.

"It looks awfully red. Nadia, can you get our first aid kit and a bowl of cold water?" Tegan requested. Nadia got up and went into the kitchen. "I think I need to speak to Lloyd alone."

"Of course. I'll be upstairs in my room," Magda said as she, Jools and Georgia got up and left the room. As they left, Nadia came in with the first aid kit and bowl of water. They placed the bowl of water on the coffee table and handed the first aid kit to Tegan.

"I've got to finish my teaching plan for tomorrow. Do you need anyone here?" Nadia asked.

"No. I'll get you if I need you," Tegan kindly refused. Nadia left, shutting the door behind her.

"Let's sit on the sofa," Tegan suggested. Her and Lloyd sat on the sofa together. Tegan opened the first aid box and got out some alcohol free sterile wipes. Focussing on helping Lloyd with his injury seemed to place her in a sort of work mode that she felt comfortable in.

"What are you doing?" Lloyd asked, confused.

"I'm going to put some wipes on those scratches," Tegan started. "Then I'll put a cold compress on your cheek to help bring potential bruising down." Tegan began putting the wipes on the scratches on Lloyd's cheek. Lloyd flinched a little.

"Are you okay with me proceeding?" Tegan asked courteously. Lloyd nodded in agreement. Tegan reached slowly to his cheek and softly cleaned the scratches. The butterflies in her stomach fluttered in excitement at her proximity to him but her head was determined to remain focussed on helping him.

"Is it bad that I want to kiss you again?" Lloyd admitted. Tegan looked at him; she impulsively wanted to answer but she managed to contain herself. After all, she thought, kissing him had landed them in this situation to begin with.

"I don't know what your girlfriend would think of that," Tegan remarked. "Aren't you running a risk being here at all?" Tegan stopped cleaning his cheek. She got out a clean cloth from the first aid kit and placed it carefully in the bowl of cold water. She squeezed as much of the water out of the cloth as she could and placed it tenderly on Lloyd's cheek.

"Hold it there for a bit," Tegan instructed him. He placed his hand over Tegan's and stroked it gently with his thumb. They looked into each other's eyes, Tegan trying not to give into her urges to kiss him. Lloyd shuffled a little closer to her.

"Tegan," Lloyd started. Before Tegan knew it, Lloyd kissed her lightly on the lips. She kissed him back tenderly. They were caught up in each other for a moment before Tegan broke away abruptly. She withdrew her hand that was on the cloth and looked away from Lloyd.

"I can't let you hurt me," Tegan croaked as she tried not to cry. "I've just gotten through a breakup where I was cheated on. I can't have you break my heart because you're under Gabriella's thumb." Lloyd turned Tegan's face to look at him.

"I'm sorry I dragged you into Gabriella's orbit of spite. I'm not with her anymore. I couldn't stay with her when I don't love her anymore. I should've left a long while ago," Lloyd apologised. Tegan felt a glimmer of hope flicker inside of her, but she didn't want to get too carried away with it.

"Okay so what if I want you too? How can we make this work with her on my tail?" Tegan asked pragmatically. Lloyd looked down at the ground, shuffling his feet. After a little while, he looked back at Tegan with conviction.

"It's your call. I don't deserve to call the shots here. It's up to you what we do," Lloyd told her. Tegan smiled at Lloyd briefly before resuming the business at hand.

"Let's not get too ahead of ourselves," Tegan decided. "I can't give you monogamy which I know you've practised before. Is that going to be okay?"

"Absolutely. Whatever you want," Lloyd quickly agreed.

"I want to know what you really want, Lloyd. Don't just blindly agree to something you may not truly want," Tegan warned him. As annoyed as she felt for the position she was in, she didn't want him to get hurt because of her. He hesitated for a moment.

"I want to be with you but I can't jump into another relationship too quickly. I want to work towards being with someone I want to be with. I've never done non-monogamy before. Is that a must?" Lloyd argued.

"Yes. I can't betray what I want, no matter how I feel about you," Tegan counter argued.

"Then I'm willing to give it a shot," Lloyd said.

"Okay," Tegan agreed. "There are three conditions to making this work."

"Name them," Lloyd asked, keen to know what she wants.

"First, we keep things casual and on the down low for now. Second, we practice polyamory and that's non-negotiable, and third, Gabriella is strictly off the table." Tegan explained. She waited for his answer with bated breath. She was concerned about his lack of experience with polyamory and her unwillingness to do anything else but her heart was ruling her actions.

"I couldn't agree more," Lloyd declared. They smiled at each other, satisfied they had come to an agreement. Lloyd held her hand again. Tegan allowed the hope she harboured to grow in her heart.

"Thank you," Lloyd said. Tegan raised her eyebrow in confusion.

"For what?" Tegan asked politely.

"For giving me a chance. I promise I won't let you down," Lloyd promised sincerely.

"Why don't we see how things go for now before making promises?" Tegan suggested. They kissed each other on the lips briefly. Tegan stood up whilst Lloyd placed the cloth back in the water bowl.

"I'm sorry, I really wish I could ask you to stay but I've got to go to bed," Tegan apologised. "Are you going to be able to get home okay? Maybe your Dad can come pick you up?" Lloyd stood up and faced her.

"Dad's probably long asleep. I'll be okay. Trust me," Lloyd tried to reassure her. Tegan smiled at him and kissed him on his uninjured cheek. As Lloyd left the house, Tegan headed up the stairs. She went to Magda's bedroom door and knocked on it. Magda opened the door, relieved to see Tegan.

"Tigs! Are you okay?" Magda asked. Nadia, Jools and Georgia crowded behind her.

"I'm okay," Tegan confirmed. Jools and Georgia came out of Magda's bedroom and into the hallway. They gathered around Tegan in a triangle which made her feel a little enclosed.

"Well?" Georgia asked.

"We're going to see how things go but we're keeping it very much on the down low," Tegan confirmed.

Trust Me

♥

T here was an awkward silence between the friends.

"That's not quite what I expected," Jools spoke up.

"Tegan, I love you but is this really a good idea?" Magda questioned.

"I made myself clear, it's all a huge 'if' and 'see where things go' situation," Tegan tried to reassure her sceptical friends.

"I get it," Georgia supported her friend.

"You do?" Tegan enquired, a little surprised.

"You like him, but you don't want to jump head first. You're putting the onus on him to prove himself worthy," Georgia theorised. Magda and Georgia nodded in agreement.

"Pretty much," Tegan agreed.

"That's a good summary," Jools complimented Georgia.

"Tegan, I may not think this is the best idea, but I'll support you one hundred percent," Magda stated.

"Thanks. I just need you to trust that I know what I'm doing," Tegan thanked Magda. They hugged each other. As they were about to separate, the other two joined in the hug.

A week had gone by, but the harassment of Tegan continued on social media with messages coming through ranging from mild irritants to threats of oncoming and serious retribution. Gabriella didn't directly message her much; she didn't need to when some of her fifteen thousand followers did it for her, but it was obvious to Tegan that they were being egged on by Gabriella's continued posts about her. Tegan couldn't help but feel somewhat paranoid about going out anywhere in case she was recognised but she resolved that she couldn't stay home out of fear.

"*I won't make Head Midwife by staying at home,*" she thought. Tegan got to her workplace on a Monday morning, ignoring the notifications on her phone in her uniform pocket. She went straight into the staff room, not saying a word to her passing colleagues. She got out a porridge pot out of her bag, filled up the kettle and put it on to boil. Unbeknownst to Tegan, Darcy came through the door. He came up to Tegan and tapped her on the shoulder. Tegan turned quickly in panic to face Darcy.

"Oh, thank goodness—it's you," Tegan said as the panic dissipated. Her heart still fluttered as she remained close to Darcy. Despite everything that had been going on, her attraction to Darcy hadn't abated.

"Did I scare you?" Darcy asked, concerned.

"No," Tegan lied initially. "I mean yes but it's not your fault. Sorry, I'm just a little jumpy." She was visibly flustered.

"What's wrong?" Darcy asked. Tegan turned away to pour the boiling water into the porridge pot. As she filled it to level, she contemplated what to say to Darcy. She was really unsure who she could trust as she felt anyone she didn't know implicitly could turn on her at any moment. Ultimately, her gut instinct told her to trust him. She turned to face Darcy again once she placed the kettle in its place.

"It's pretty complicated," Tegan explained. "Are you sure you have the time?"

"I might not right now," Darcy conceded. "But perhaps we should meet for coffee sometime to chat?" Tegan was taken aback by his directness but impressed, nonetheless. It was rare that anyone was that direct with her, but she enjoyed it all the same.

"I think that's a reasonable solution," Tegan agreed with a half-smile. Darcy smiled back at her.

"Okay. My shift is almost over. Once I've had some sleep, I could text you?" Darcy suggested.

"Don't you need my number for that?" Tegan pointed out cheekily. Her cheeky turn surprised her, but she was too exhilarated to care.

"Good point." Darcy got out a piece of paper and pen from his pocket and handed them to Tegan. She wrote down her number and handed it back to him. He placed it in the pocket of his shirt.

"I'll text you later, Ms Javaman," Darcy coolly said as he walked out of the staff room. Tegan turned back to her porridge pot, smiling from ear to ear. It almost made her forget entirely about the situation with Lloyd and Gabriella as she stirred her breakfast. A sense of worry kicked in:

"*Is he simply just being friendly? Was I too forward earlier and did he relent out of obligation? Am I misreading the entire situation?*" She was so lost in her thoughts she briefly forgot about her porridge. She looked down at it. She decided to try and stop thinking too hard about anything other than work. With that, she grabbed her breakfast and began to eat it. As she ate, she started to think about the clinic ahead, all the pregnant people she'd see, and what could come up that'll distract her mind.

It was 7pm and the end of Tegan's shift. She checked her phone notifications. Among the slew of notifications from social media, there was one text message notification from Darcy. She grinned, happy he followed through. She put her phone back in the pocket of her uniform. As she headed for the entrance, she was stopped by a blonde woman in a grey power suit. This turned her good mood into one of trepidation.

"Tegan Javaman," The woman greeted her coldly. "I'm Sharon McDonald, the head of the maternity ward at this hospital. Please come with me." The woman escorted Tegan into a small office, out of the way from the hustle and bustle of the ward. Tegan tried to get a read as to what was going on but didn't feel successful. When they got into the office, Tegan took a seat opposite Sharon. She started fidgeting with her hands in a stimming manner to try and calm herself down.

"How can I help you?" Tegan asked politely. Sharon produced an envelope addressed to her which confused Tegan.

"Someone posted this offensive material to me. Do you have any knowledge of this?" Sharon explained as she slid the envelope over to Tegan. She tentatively opened it: it contained images of Tegan's head superimposed on illegal and offensive pornographic imagery. The blood drained from Tegan's face in total fear. Gabriella had figured out where she worked and was using it as a means of terror. She felt the goosebumps raise on her arms. She faced Sharon, trying not to cry.

"This isn't me! I have no idea what this is!" Tegan truthfully exclaimed. Sharon reached across the desk, placed the images back in the envelope and put them back in a drawer. Her steely expression frightened Tegan as she couldn't figure out where the conversation was going.

"One of my sons works in graphic design," Sharon brought up. "He wasn't born great, but he certainly has a talent for it." Tegan looked at Sharon confused, wondering how this was at all relevant to what she had just been shown.

"The content of the imagery notwithstanding, this level of design wouldn't pass a GCSE Graphic Design assignment," Sharon explained.

"So..." Tegan hesitated, hopeful. "You know these are fakes?"

"Of course, but I'm alarmed that something like this would come to me to begin with. It's not every day you get that sort of material coming to your desk," Sharon told her. "Is there anything you'd like to share with me?" Tegan thought about it for a moment. She could tell her boss's boss everything that was going on, but it didn't feel right. She wasn't sure she'd even be believed if she wasn't dismissed out of hand. She was still alarmed that Gabriella found out where she worked, and the fear of consequences still ruled her head. She ultimately shook her head, deciding not to reveal anything to her boss's boss.

"Okay. If anything like this happens again, I will be forced to take action. Do you understand?" Sharon asked. Tegan understood what she meant, and whilst she didn't enjoy the perceived inference she was to blame in any way, she was just relieved she wasn't in any actual trouble yet.

"Crystal clear," Tegan confirmed.

The Reaction

♥

Tegan came through the door of her house, feeling a mixture of happiness and concern. She closed the door behind her. She took off her shoes and placed them on the shoe rack. She went up the stairs to get into her bedroom. As she got into her bedroom, she started taking off her uniform.

"Don't stop," A voice uttered from her bed. She turned suddenly to see Lloyd lying on her bed with a bunch of daffodils in a vase. A smile stretched across her face. She kept her uniform on for the time being.

"What are you doing here?" Tegan asked with a smile across her face.

"Seeing as we can't go out to a restaurant, I thought I'd bring the restaurant to us," Lloyd answered, shaking his phone lightly which had UberEats open. Tegan, touched by his thoughtfulness, came to the bed and kissed him.

"Just what I needed after today," Tegan admitted as she sat on the bed. Lloyd sat up and cuddled her. She felt his warm embrace permeate through her like a blanket on a winter's night.

"What happened at work today?" Lloyd queried.

"Gabriella sent in rather crudely photoshopped images of me doing some rather horrendous things to the head of maternity," Tegan told him, facing him as she did. Lloyd was dismayed but kept calm.

"I take it you didn't lose your job?" Lloyd wondered hopefully.

"Oh no. Thankfully she saw right through it but made it clear she's not amused," Tegan answered. She looked deep into his light blue eyes and smiled.

"She's not going to defeat us," Tegan told him with determination. "She can try and ruin me all she wants but she won't get what she wants."

"I know. I just don't want her to ruin your career."

"She's not going to ruin my career. Besides, with her increasingly unhinged social media posts, I have half a mind to go to the Police for harassment."

"You should. It might not stop her, though."

"Honestly? I just find the idea of her in a cell or being interrogated without Daddy bailing her out funny." They laughed together. Tegan took Lloyd's phone from his hand playfully. She started looking through what to eat on the UberEats app. After a moment of browsing, she spotted something she was interested in.

"I fancy Chinese. How about you?" Tegan suggested.

"I fancy a bit of you first," Lloyd flirted. Tegan placed the phone on her bedside table and snogged him. They were getting wrapped up in their passion with their hands all over each other. Lloyd's hands started to caress Tegan's work tunic, unzipping it from the front. Tegan started to take it off and—

"MAGDA!" Nadia screamed from downstairs. Tegan and Lloyd got off each other, ran out of her bedroom and raced downstairs to see Magda struggling to breathe. She dropped an envelope on the floor.

"What's going on?" Lloyd asked, scared of what was going on. Nadia faced the pair as Tegan zipped her tunic up.

"Someone's sent a letter with peanuts inside," Nadia cried, losing their usual sense of calm. Tegan faced Magda again whose face was swelling fast. She grabbed the envelope and saw the peanuts in the envelope. She placed it away from Magda.

"It's anaphylaxis! Lloyd, call an ambulance. Nadia, get Magda's Epi-Pen. She has one in the First Aid box," Tegan instructed. Nadia rushed to the kitchen to find the First Aid box whilst Tegan handed Lloyd her mobile phone. As Lloyd made the call to 999, Tegan turned to Magda. Inside, she was terrified at what was happening to her friend but knew she had to maintain her composure, so she'd remember what to do and not alarm those around her.

"Magda, I need you to go down on the ground," Tegan told her calmly. They went down on the floor together, both sitting upright.

"Now, stay sitting up if you can. Nadia will be here with the EpiPen in a second," Tegan tried to reassure her. Tegan could clearly see that Magda was scared as Lloyd was on the phone to 999. Nadia rushed back into the room with an EpiPen. They handed it to Tegan who quickly took off the blue safety cap.

"Okay, blue to sky, orange to thigh," Tegan muttered to herself as she positioned the EpiPen roughly ten centimetres away from Magda's inner thigh. She was both scared at the rapid way Magda had reacted to the peanuts and at the idea of not succeeding in helping her best friend. Without thinking about it any further, she jabbed the pen into Magda's outer thigh and held it firmly for three seconds as it injected her with adrenaline. She took the EpiPen out of Magda's thigh and turned to Lloyd.

"How's the ambulance coming along?" Tegan asked him.

"They're on their way. Did you use the EpiPen?" Lloyd answered.

"Yes, just now. Let them know to be ready with another one just in case," Tegan replied with authority. She turned back to face Magda whose breathing was improving.

"You getting there, Mags?" Nadia asked shakily.

"Yeah," Magda said, still catching her breath. "Thanks."

"Nadia, get rid of the peanuts," Tegan instructed them. Nadia grabbed the envelope and went into the kitchen. There was a loud knock on the door. Tegan jumped up from the floor.

"I better get it," said Tegan. "You stay with Magda. If she gets worse, get me," Tegan instructed Lloyd. Tegan went straight to the hallway and the front door. She opened it to see two paramedics at the door with a stretcher and another Epi-Pen.

"We're here for the anaphylaxis," The first paramedic greeted her. Tegan breathed a sigh of relief.

"Come straight in." Tegan showed them to the living room, straight to Magda who was still on the floor. Lloyd hung up the phone and handed it back to Tegan who placed her phone in her tunic. Whilst the paramedics worked on Magda, Nadia came back into the room with a letter.

"Tegan, I just read what was in the letter. I think you might want to read it too," Nadia told Tegan, handing her the letter. She opened the letter that read 'Enjoy my tasty treat.' She recognised the handwriting; it was undeniably Gabriella's doing. Tegan folded the paper back and handed it to Nadia.

"Put it somewhere safe. I'm calling the Police as soon as Magda is gone," Tegan resolved, gritting her teeth in barely contained rage. Nadia ran to their bedroom. Anger boiled within Tegan.

"She may come after me all she likes," Tegan said, her voice shaking with rage. "But coming after the people I love is something else. I want to see that woman pay." Lloyd put an arm around Tegan, but she brushed him off. She took a breath and composed herself.

"You better go. If she tracks us down, at best she's going to cause a scene if you're around," Tegan requested. Lloyd nodded, kissed her forehead and went upstairs. He passed Nadia who came down the stairs. They came back into the living room. The paramedics got Magda onto the stretcher.

"We've got space for one of you to come in the ambulance with us," The first paramedic told Nadia and Tegan.

"I think it should be you, Nadia. I'll come up in a taxi once I've spoken to the Police," Tegan suggested. Nadia nodded in agreement. The paramedics, Magda and Nadia left the house as Lloyd came down the stairs. He turned to face Tegan who started getting her shoes on.

"Let me know when you get home?" Tegan asked sweetly. Lloyd nodded then walked away. As he shut the door, Tegan's started to break. A singular tear rolled down her face as she took in everything that happened. She clenched her fists, trying to suppress her fear and upset at the situation.

The Aftermath

♥

It was 10pm: Tegan went into the Colton City hospital cafeteria. It was relatively quiet with the clatter of cutlery being washed in the kitchen and the smell of old coffee being brewed for sleep deprived hospital workers. Tegan wandered through the cafeteria aimlessly. She eventually picked up a ham & cheese sandwich and a bottle of Fanta from the fridge. She also got a packet of crisps. She didn't particularly want to eat but she knew she hadn't for quite some time. It was very different to the Chinese takeaway she envisioned eating with Lloyd, but it would have to do for the time being. She approached the cashier to pay. She scrambled to get her debit card out of her wallet until she heard:

"I've got it," a silky-smooth voice softly offered gently. Tegan turned to face them. It was Darcy who was dressed in a t-shirt and jeans. Tegan was speechless for a moment as he gave the cashier his food and debit card. He was the last person she expected to see but she was glad to see him.

"What are you doing here?" Darcy asked innocently as he got his debit card and food back. The cashier handed Tegan her food as she gathered herself enough to speak.

"I could ask you the same thing," Tegan pointed out. "Aren't you meant to be having the day off?"

"I had to come in but I just finished. The life of a trainee consultant!" Darcy explained.

"Oh, that sucks," Tegan replied as they headed to the tables. They sat at a table with two seats opposite each other.

"You never answered why you're here," Darcy asked as he sat on the chair. Tegan began to stim with her hands and her right leg shook a little.

"We got sent a letter with peanuts in it. One of my housemates has a deadly contact allergy to peanuts and she opened the letter." Tegan sighed.

"Who on Earth would do that?" Darcy asked, aggrieved at such a thing.

"The guy I'm seeing has an abusive ex-girlfriend who seems to think I ruined her life because he left her," Tegan summarised. Darcy looked taken aback by Tegan's statement.

"Did he leave her for you?" he challenged her.

"I did mention the abusive bit, right?" Tegan deflected, a little annoyed at the insinuation.

"You did, but you didn't answer my question." Darcy's eyes seemingly penetrated Tegan's defensive armour with a look. Tegan sighed and started to unscrew her Fanta bottle so her hands would have something else to do.

"He didn't leave her for me, but we did start seeing each other casually in secret after he did," Tegan explained honestly. There was a pause between them as Tegan waited with anticipation for his response. She fidgeted with her Fanta bottle cap, nervous at what he might now think of her for this.

"Fair enough. I hope he's escaped her for good," Darcy said diplomatically. Tegan raised her eyebrow.

"What do you mean?" Tegan asked, confused.

"She may be going after you but it sounds as if she wants him back. I don't want you to go through another heartbreak," Darcy explained. The admission surprised Tegan: he always seemed so cool, charming and above it all to her. It never seemed to occur to her that he might care about her as a human being.

"I'll be okay," Tegan tried to reassure him. She smiled at him with a sense of longing usually reserved for someone in a relationship.

"Besides," Tegan started to joke, "being polyamorous means I'll just jump back into someone else's bed in no time. That's what the monogamous lot say, right?"

"I didn't realise you were polyamorous too." Darcy laughed. Tegan shot him a defiant smile, determined to enjoy this interaction.

"You learn something new every day," Tegan teased him.

A while later, Tegan came back alone into the Majors section of the Accident & Emergency department. She felt happy after her conversation with Darcy but still concerned about what landed Magda in the hospital that night. She approached Magda's bay where she had an oxygen mask on and was connected to an IV of antihistamines and cortisol. Her face and hands were still rather swollen but less so than they were before. She was alone asleep but roused awake when she heard Tegan come by.

"Tigs!" Magda croaked. Tegan went to her and carefully held her swollen hand, making sure she didn't hurt her any further.

"How're you feeling?"

"Better," Magda quietly replied, fiddling with her oxygen mask.

"Keep that mask on until the doctor says otherwise," Tegan said. Magda stopped fiddling with the oxygen mask to talk.

"Tegan! You're back!" Nadia exclaimed as they came back.

"Where have you been?" Georgia asked, bringing up the rear. They stood beside Magda opposite Tegan. She was a little reluctant to explain where she had been, but she didn't want to lie to them.

"I bumped into a colleague in the cafeteria, and we got chatting," Tegan said.

"Is that the hot consultant bloke?" Nadia asked bluntly. Tegan looked around then looked back at Nadia, embarrassed. Georgia picked up on it.

"There was surely a more subtle way of saying that, right Nadia?" Georgia intervened.

"Sorry Tegan," Nadia said.

"It's fine." Tegan sighed.

"You should invite him to the Shaky Martini reopening next week," Nadia suggested.

"Yeah! I know you would've wanted to bring Lloyd but—" Georgia started. There was an awkward silence for a brief moment whilst Tegan picked up on Georgia' intended inference.

"I get you. You don't want an incident with Gabriella at your work's big party. That's fair enough, Georgia. I'm sure Lloyd would understand," Tegan reassured her.

"Thank you for understanding," said Georgia.

"I'm not sure Darcy would want to come. That would be a bit odd, wouldn't it?" Tegan wondered.

"Not necessarily," Georgia said.

"If it makes you feel better, you can always invite a couple of other colleagues along. Right, Georgia?" Nadia pointed out.

"Just invite him!" Magda croaked through her oxygen mask.

"Thanks everyone." Tegan smiled at her friends. She yawned, covering her mouth as she did so. The extent of her exhaustion hit her like a cacophony of bricks hitting her.

"You better get some sleep, Tegan. You've not had a rest since you got home from work," Nadia mentioned.

"I've got to get back to Jools and Carla but I'd be happy to drop you off on the way," Georgia suggested.

"Will you be okay if I leave?" Tegan asked Magda. She nodded at her. Tegan stroked Magda's hand briefly before leaving the room with Georgia.

This Is About Justice

♥

An hour later, Tegan got into her home. She was struck by the silence of her surroundings with the exception of the slight hum of the refrigerator in the kitchen. She took her shoes off gently and placed them on the shoe rack. She rushed up the stairs and stormed into her bedroom, slamming the door behind her. Tears pricked in her eyes as the events of the past several hours truly sunk in. She did her best not to cry out, but a tear trickled down her face. She rustled her work tunic and got out a tissue. She dabbed her eyes gently as she continued to resist the urge to fully cry. As she tried to get herself together, there was a knock on the front door. The sudden noise made her jump and snap into action. She headed down the stairs and opened the door: it was Lloyd. Tegan was relieved to see him but felt a little annoyed she hadn't had any space to fully breathe. Nonetheless, she let him in and closed the door quickly behind him.

"Sorry I know I should've called first but you didn't respond to my texts," Lloyd explained as he faced Tegan.

"I just got back from the hospital," Tegan told him as she turned to face him. She placed her left hand over herself and held on to the opposite arm.

"Is Magda going to be okay?" Lloyd asked with concern.

"She'll be fine eventually. She'll likely be in the hospital until late tomorrow," Tegan answered.

"What did the Police say?" he asked.

"They're waiting for Magda to be in a better state before interviewing us. I don't know why they couldn't just speak to us now and wait for Magda but that's beyond me," Tegan said. She sighed and began to fidget with her work tunic awkwardly. Lloyd put his arm around Tegan: he could sense what was up with her without having to ask.

"It's not your fault," Lloyd tried to reassure her.

"Yeah. My friend is in the hospital because magical pixies sent her nuts," Tegan sarcastically retorted. She pulled herself away from Lloyd and went into the living room. She sat on the sofa and put her face in her hands. Lloyd came through and sat next to her. He placed his arm around her and brought her to him. She placed her hands on him as he started to stroke her auburn hair. She felt comfortable in his embrace.

"This isn't your fault. I'm the one who broke up with her," Lloyd said to try and soothe her.

"And yet she's targeting me and my friends," Tegan pointed out sadly. "She could've killed Magda. She almost did."

"I don't know why her retribution is aimed at you, but she won't succeed. I know I screwed up in all this, but I refuse to stop seeing you," Lloyd tried to reassure her. Tegan moved her head and faced Lloyd. They were about to kiss when a loud knocking was heard at the front door. Tegan got up quickly and raced to the front door, fuelled by adrenaline. She opened the door: it was Gabriella whose initial smugness turned to confusion. She was holding her phone up, obviously filming Tegan. Tegan's rage bubbled on the surface, but she tried to contain it as much as she could. After all: she didn't want to give Gabriella or her devoted followers a reason to get any satisfaction.

"What the hell are you doing here?" Tegan asked curtly.

"Aren't you supposed to be sick?" Gabriella indignantly enquired, visibly annoyed that Tegan was healthy.

"Magda is the one allergic to peanuts and your little stunt could've killed her," Tegan said furiously.

"Where's Lloyd?" Gabriella demanded, swiftly changing the subject. She moved a step forward, preparing to move into Tegan's house.

"He's not here."

"I want to see."

"Absolutely not! You've already violated my home by almost killing one of my best friends, set your fanbase after me on false information, and tried to get me fired from my job with forged pornography. Over what? Some dude who broke up with you? Isn't that pathetic?" Tegan pointed out angrily. Gabriella tried to barge her way through, but Tegan impulsively pushed her back. There was no way Gabriella was going to get into the house for now.

"I'll have you for assault!" Gabriella screamed.

"The Police have already been informed about what happened to Magda. You do anything anywhere near my home again and I'll ensure Daddy won't be able to bail you out," Tegan warned. Gabriella moved the phone away from Tegan and pressed a button on her screen. She put it back in her purse and spat at the ground towards Tegan's feet and walked away. Tegan slammed the door shut and ran into the living room where Lloyd was standing, concerned. She turned her back to the door and leaned against it. Her heart was racing out of fear and anger. She was a little satisfied she didn't completely lose it but was worried about what might come next. She felt the anxiety course through her veins but did her best to calm down. After a moment, she went back into the living room to a concerned and anxious Lloyd.

"Thanks for not coming out. She was filming me," Tegan explained as she sat back down on the sofa next to Lloyd.

"I imagine she wants to keep her fans entertained," Lloyd cynically remarked.

"This is too vindictive to be entertainment," Tegan mentioned. "This is about justice in her eyes. What are we going to do?"

"We need to tell the Police everything if you haven't already. They need to understand how serious this is getting," Lloyd answered.

"I told them everything. Their solution seems to be waiting around," Tegan complained. "I know this sounds crazy, but I'm worried someone is going to get hurt worse than Magda did tonight," Tegan fretted. Lloyd put his arm around Tegan again.

"Don't worry Tegan. I'm sure no one will let it get that far. Gabriella might be particularly unhinged but she's not a murderer," Lloyd tried to reassure her. Tegan shot a small smile to try and appease him but in her heart, she couldn't shake the feeling something worse was coming.

The next morning at 11am, an exhausted Tegan was preparing to start her shift at Colton City Hospital. She brushed her hair and tied it in a ponytail in front of her locker in the locker room. She put the hairbrush back in her locker along with her handbag. She put her mobile phone in the work tunic she was wearing. She took a deep breath, composed herself and left the locker room feeling slightly ready to tackle the day ahead. She went on to the ward, determined to get through her shift. She encountered Sinead who appeared to be in a particularly good mood.

"Tegan! Good to see you," Sinead greeted her. "I believe we'll start by—" She was interrupted by a woman rushing into the room with panic in her eyes.

"I need help!" the woman screamed as she ran out again. Sinead and Tegan looked at each other briefly before following the woman. They caught up to the woman as they ended up in the waiting area of the Maternity department. Tegan quickly realised what was going on; her heavily pregnant sister, Sara, was struggling in pain with someone incoherently screaming at her on the phone. Tegan froze as Sinead rushed to Sara and started to help her. Sinead turned to face Tegan, wondering why Tegan hadn't come to help.

"Tegan, I need you to help," Sinead asked as she tried to soothe Sara. Tegan snapped into action, determined to help Sara regardless of how she felt herself. Tegan realised someone was still screaming at Sara on the phone. Tegan took the phone away from Sara's hand and disconnected the call. She put the phone in her work tunic to keep it safe.

Squash The Nonsense

♥

"What's going on, Sara?" Tegan asked her softly. Sara faced her sister.

"Something doesn't feel right, Tegan. The pain—" Sara started as another surge of pain went through her abdomen.

"We need to get you on a bed and properly monitored," Sinead explained to Sara. Tegan and Sinead both helped Sara up. As they got her up, Tegan noticed pink fluid from where Sara sat. She knew what this meant; Sara's water had broken early.

"Sinead, her waters have broken and there's blood," Tegan said.

"Let's just get her on a bed, Tegan," Sinead pressed as they continued to move Sara.

"Sinead, she's not due yet. She's only 32 weeks along," Tegan explained urgently.

"How do you know?" Sinead asked as they got to the beds.

"Tegan is my younger sister," Sara panted as she got on to an empty ward bed. Sinead got a blood pressure machine and placed the cuff on

Sara's arm. Sinead pressed the button to start measuring Sara's blood pressure.

"Tegan—" Sara started.

"Don't talk. You need to try and keep as calm and still as possible," Tegan softly said to her. The blood pressure machine was done measuring; it was high at 146/100.

"Sara, I'm going to need you to do a urine sample. Tegan, make sure you grab one of the other midwives. We're going to need to be ready for anything and you can't be the one treating your sister," Sinead instructed. She went to get a pot for Sara. Tegan was about to walk out when Sara grabbed her arm. She turned to face her older sister, wondering what she was about to say.

"It's okay, I'll be back, and we'll get you sorted out," Tegan tried to reassure Sara.

"Tegan, it was Gabriella screaming at me on the phone," Sara explained. "I don't know how she got my number, but you need to get this nonsense squashed." Tegan's heart dropped. The overwhelming guilt she felt rushed in her head.

"*How could I have been so selfish as to cause my sister's early labour?*" she thought to herself. She quickly snapped out of it on the outside as she pushed forward.

"Let's focus on getting you sorted. Sinead will be back in a moment with a urine pot, and I'll be back with another midwife," Tegan said. She squeezed her hand briefly as a reassuring gesture before letting go to run and get someone.

Twelve hours went by. Tegan sat in the relatives room, clutching a cup of coffee in her hand, still dressed in her work uniform. There were thoughts of guilt and shame ruminating around her head. She couldn't stop thinking about the fact that Gabriella had got a hold of her sister's number. How? Who would be next on her hit list? Will the Police act? As she got lost in her thoughts, Darcy came through the door dressed in scrubs looking for her. Tegan stood up, prepared to await whatever news was coming.

"Tegan. There you are," Darcy greeted her as he approached her.

"Any news?" Tegan asked, concerned.

"You have a baby nephew. He's in the neonatal intensive care unit for monitoring but the prognosis is good for him," Darcy told her. Tegan placed the cup of coffee on the nearby table. She could hardly believe she got a bit of good news, but she wasn't prepared to celebrate yet.

"And Sara?" she asked.

"She's sleeping. I know you know enough about preeclampsia to know that she needs monitoring for a while, but I think she'll be okay," Darcy answered. Tegan sighed in relief, feeling the tension melt away a little from her mind knowing both her sister and nephew were okay. She all but collapsed back down on the chair she was sitting on, and Darcy sat on a chair next to her.

"How's Magda?" Darcy asked gently. Tegan looked at him.

"She's home. She's still a bit swollen but that'll be gone soon enough," Tegan answered.

"What did the Police say?"

"They haven't bothered speaking to me yet but apparently they've spoken to Magda and Nadia. They said they're looking into the Magda incident. I'm still waiting for the police officer to get back to me about when they're going to get my statement."

"Wait, so they haven't even spoken to the person who put in the report? That's ridiculous."

"Yep. Meanwhile I have to wait and see what else Gabriella is going to pull besides the social media harassment, almost killing my best friend with peanuts, and trying to get me fired from work with false nudes."

"All in the space of what—a couple of weeks?"

"Something like that. Give her this: her campaign is relentless. I just don't know what I'm going to do." Darcy placed his hand on Tegan's leg. The feeling that surged in Tegan was like a rush in spite of her exhausted, stressed out state.

"I know we haven't known each other long but just know I'm here for you," Darcy told Tegan. Tegan smiled a half smile at him. She felt so grateful towards him for not only being consistently kind to her regardless of the situation but for not judging her for her actions.

"Thank you," Tegan said to him.

"It's nothing," Darcy insisted.

"I mean it," Tegan said as she impulsively placed her hand on his. "Thank you." After a moment, Darcy held her hand. They looked at each other, unsure of what was going to happen next. Would they kiss? After a few seconds, the door opened. Darcy and Tegan withdrew their hands quickly. A woman neither of them knew came through the door with two men. Darcy and Tegan stood up.

"Oh, sorry, I—" the woman started.

"Don't worry. This is the relatives room. You can come in," Tegan interrupted.

"We were just leaving," Darcy elaborated. At that, he and Tegan quickly went past the trio and left the relatives room. Darcy closed the door behind them to allow the trio some privacy.

"I better get going. I should've left a while ago to relieve the babysitter," Darcy told Tegan.

"Yeah I better get home and get some sleep," Tegan mentioned. Darcy started to walk away which is when Tegan summoned some courage she hadn't had yet.

"Darcy!" she called out to him. He turned back to face her as she approached him.

"One of my best friends manages The Shaky Martini. It's the re-opening night on Saturday and I wondered if you'd come along with me?" Tegan impulsively asked. Darcy stepped towards Tegan again. Tegan's heart pounded out of her chest in anticipation for his answer. She dreaded a rejection, but she knew she couldn't take back what she'd said.

"I'm sure I can find someone to look after Beth that night. You're in tomorrow, right?" Darcy asked coolly.

"Yes. I'll get the details from Georgia before my shift," Tegan confirmed.

"I'm in, then," Darcy agreed.

"Okay." Tegan smiled as he walked away. Her heart raced as she walked in the opposite direction, happy to have asked and hanging on to the positive for once.

A Smelly Welcome

♥

Midnight struck and Tegan came through her front door, exhausted but happy after her long day. She messily kicked off her shoes and placed her coat on the nearby hanger. She was about to head up the stairs when Nadia and Magda came out of the living room, concerned and a little annoyed with Tegan.

"You're home!" a still slightly swollen Magda shouted out.

"How's your sister?" Nadia asked.

"You didn't text us back!" Magda continued. Tegan felt bombarded which she didn't appreciate but she could understand where they were coming from.

"I'm sorry. I just—" Tegan apologised as she approached the two. "I'm sorry. She's going to be okay. She gave birth to a boy." Suddenly, Magda hugged Tegan tightly which threw her off guard.

"That's so awesome. Do you have a picture of the little man?" Magda asked excitedly as she broke away from a flustered Tegan.

"Not yet. I'll see him in the Neonatal Intensive Care Unit before my shift starts tomorrow," Tegan replied.

"Is he going to be okay?" Magda enquired.

"He's got a good prognosis, but we'll know more tomorrow," Tegan answered with a smile, remembering how she asked Darcy out to an event. Nadia spotted this seemingly out of character, oddly timed smile and became suspicious.

"What's with the smile?" Nadia asked.

"Darcy agreed to come with me to The Shaky Martini reopening on Saturday," Tegan started excitedly. "I know it's not the thing to dwell on right now -"

"It's absolutely fine to be happy about this," Magda interrupted.

"Yeah. You've been through so much crap lately. You deserve a win," Nadia joined in. "How're you feeling, Tegan?" All of the questions were ebbing away at Tegan's excited nature along with her general exhaustion.

"Right now? Exhausted and overwhelmed," Tegan responded. "I need to get some sleep before tomorrow's shift."

"When are you next seeing Lloyd?" Magda asked. Tegan suppressed the need to sigh. She just wanted to get some sleep and not be interrogated anymore.

"He's coming over tomorrow after work. I'll tell him about Saturday then," Tegan replied. With that, she turned away from her housemates and went up the stairs to her bedroom. She took off her work uniform and into her pyjamas. She got her mobile phone out of her work tunic, set her alarm for the next day and placed it on her bedside table. She slowly started to fall asleep, somewhat content for the first time in a while.

The following night arrived, and Tegan was walking home wearing a dark cardigan over her work uniform. She wandered towards her home but just as she was about to step towards the door, she spotted a poorly disguised collection of dog faeces in plastic dog poop bags. She sighed out of complete frustration and got her phone out. She took a photo of the offending mess then called Nadia, hoping they'd be in the house. As soon as the call went to voicemail, Tegan disconnected it and tried to call Magda. When that didn't work, she got out her keys and carefully tread over the pile of dog poop to get into her house. She immediately headed for her kitchen, grabbed a bin liner, put on washing up gloves, and went straight back to the dog poo. As she disposed of the disgusting pile in a bin bag, Lloyd approached her. Tegan turned to see him standing there looking puzzled.

"Do I need to ask?" said Lloyd.

"I think this is too much of a biohazard to be your ex girlfriend's doing," Tegan surmised as she tied the bin liner up. "I suspect it's a fan of hers."

"How did they find your address?" Lloyd asked in a concerned tone as Tegan put the bin liner in the black wheelie bin.

"I can't prove that it's her but on the other hand, it's hardly likely to be anyone else," Tegan said as she put the washing up gloves in the bin. Lloyd went to hug her but Tegan stopped him.

"Let's wait for me to wash my hands first," Tegan requested. "Then I'm all yours." Tegan and Lloyd went into her home, shutting the door quickly behind them. Tegan rushed to the kitchen to wash her hands. As she did so, Lloyd followed her in.

"Do you want to come down to The Purifier on Saturday night? My band will be playing from 9pm and I'd love to see you there," Lloyd asked. Tegan finished washing her hands and faced Lloyd.

"I'm sorry but are you really sure me going to one of your gigs is a good idea with Gabriella on the loose?" Tegan questioned. "Besides, I've already got plans to go to The Shaky Martini that night for its reopening."

"Oh yeah," Lloyd said, shuffling uncomfortably. "I forgot about that. Are you going with the girls and Nadia?"

"Yes, and I've asked Darcy to come with me," Tegan admitted.

"Who's he?" Lloyd asked.

"He's the trainee consultant I'm friends with at work," Tegan replied. "I've told you about him." A silence fell between the pair, causing Tegan to feel anxious over what Lloyd might say next.

"Ah." Lloyd hesitated. "I see how it is."

"Don't get annoyed. You know full well Gabriella would more than ruin it if we're seen in public together," Tegan reminded him.

"I know but another man—really?" Lloyd protested.

"Lloyd, we're not being monogamous. Besides, it's not like that with Darcy. I'm pretty sure we'll just be friends. Your jealousy isn't founded," Tegan pointed out. She placed her hand on Lloyd's cheek tenderly. Lloyd turned and kissed her hand.

"I'm sorry," he said. "I'm just not used to this."

"To what?" Tegan asked.

"Any of this. I don't know how to handle something open," Lloyd lamented. Tegan kissed him on the cheek and held his hands.

"You just have to take it one step at a time," Tegan explained. "Just like we said we would." Lloyd kissed her soap-scented hands.

"I'm sorry, Tegan. I'll work on it. I promise," he promised to her.

It was the following day, and Tegan was at work tending to a patient. As she wrote down notes, Tegan couldn't help but feel uneasy at what Lloyd had said the night before. Whilst it was a semi common experience for her to feel uneasy, this feeling felt a bit different. She had a flash of doubt she hadn't felt before; she briefly wondered if her and Lloyd could make things work.

"*It's just crap getting to me*," she resolved to herself as she put the notes back. "*Let's just crack on with the day*." She smiled at her patient, turned away and walked out the door looking for Sinead. She walked past colleagues as she hunted for her supervisor. She wandered into the reception area to find Sinead talking with the receptionist.

"Sinead!" Tegan called out. Sinead faced Tegan and went towards her.

"Tegan! Everything okay?" Sinead asked.

"Yeah. I finished the notes up," Tegan answered. "The patient seems okay in there."

"Perfect. Let's head back and see if Dr Birch and his trainees have come back," Sinead proposed. They walked together back into the ward where a plethora of labour & delivery rooms lay with midwives delivering children into the world. Tegan was in her element in this place and felt relatively safe in the clinical enviornment. Sure, there were occasional dramas but nothing that she couldn't handle. Sinead and Tegan entered a private labour & delivery room only to encounter an unwelcome guest; Gabriella handing over a leaflet to a patient who looked very confused. Tegan froze in place, angry and frightened, as Gabriella faced her and Sinead.

What Do You Call It?

♥

"Well, if it isn't the fat slag herself," Gabriella taunted as she headed towards Tegan. Sinead headed to the patient to take the leaflet away as Tegan stayed to face Gabriella. Unbeknownst to Tegan, Darcy and a couple of other trainee consultants walked into the nearby corridor.

"I'm going to get what I want eventually, Javaman," Gabriella teased. "I'm going to get my revenge and I'm going to get Lloyd back. Just wait and see." Tegan refused to say anything back which started to visibly annoy Gabriella.

"Nothing to say, fatso? What are you, scared?" Gabriella shouted as she got in Tegan's face. Darcy started moving towards Tegan when she finally spoke.

"Oh no, you threatened me for the thousandth time and called me fat," Tegan remarked sarcastically. "You were more imaginative with your insults back at school. Has the coke corroded your brain cells or something?"

"I'll get you!" Gabriella screamed. Gabriella was about to slap Tegan in the face but Darcy grabbed her and moved her back, causing Gabriella to miss. Darcy kept a hold of Tegan as Gabriella started to walk away.

"Someone get Security," Darcy commanded. "That woman is wanted by Police." The other two trainees rushed away as Sinead went back to Tegan, holding the leaflet.

"Are you okay Tegan?" Sinead asked. Tegan's heart was racing, not just from the confrontation but from Darcy's tight hold. Her mind couldn't grip itself on to a comprehensive thought for a moment. Tears started to form in her eyes much to her chagrin.

"Yeah," Tegan croaked. "I'll be fine. What was in the leaflet?"

"You don't want to know," Sinead hesitated.

"Tegan needs to tell the Police," Darcy reminded Sinead. "She should probably know what's in it." Sinead sighed and handed it over to Tegan.

"I'll give you some time to call the Police in the staff room," Sinead explained as Tegan took the leaflet. "I'm going to make sure none of the other patients received any such material." Sinead went back towards the other antenatal rooms whilst Tegan tried her best not to cry. Darcy stepped away from her as she walked away.

It was 9pm and the end of Tegan's shift. She sat in her work uniform on her own in the staff changing room, trying to compose herself long enough to leave without bursting into tears. She was exhausted, frustrated, and apprehensive.

"If she can get to me at work and at home, where am I safe?" Tegan wondered to herself. She let out a sigh, slapped her legs, and went up to her locker. She opened it and grabbed a t-shirt and trousers. She changed her trousers and unzipped her nursing tunic. As she started to

put her t-shirt on, she heard the door open. She turned as she put her t-shirt over her chest and tummy. It was Darcy, who started to blush slightly at seeing Tegan in a state of undress.

"Oh crap," Tegan started. "I'm so sorry."

"Don't apologise. It is a changing room," he tried to assure her as she put her shoes on. "I was hoping to find you."

"Oh?" Tegan began as she stood up to grab a bag out of her locker and shut it.

"I wanted to make sure you were okay, that's all," Darcy explained. "What happened with the Police?" Tegan shut the locker door and locked it before turning to face Darcy again.

"They did what they always do: ask the same questions, took the leaflet, said they'd get back to me," Tegan said, feeling very defeated by the whole ordeal.

"Is that it? She almost assaulted you at work. Someone's got to do something to stop her."

"Allegedly, the Police will do that but the longer this goes on, the more unhinged she gets," Tegan lamented. She could feel in herself that she wanted to cry but she was trying her best not to: after all, she didn't want to appear vulnerable in front of Darcy. She stared at the floor, trying her best to refrain from crying. He approached her slowly and held her shoulders.

"I'm sorry. I wish I could do something to make you feel better," he admitted to her. Tegan looked up at him, feeling exhilarated by his touch. He brought her in for a hug and she held onto him. In the moment, she felt safe and excited by the person holding her; she wanted to stay like that for as long as possible. After a minute, they started to slowly pull away from each other. They stopped as their faces were in close proximity to each other. Tegan wasn't sure what to do; a part of her badly wanted to kiss him, a part of her felt like it wasn't the right time to do so. The decision was made for her as the door started to open again. They leapt away from each other as a pair of midwives came unsuspectingly through the door.

"I best be going," Tegan declared as her mind came back to Earth and the midwives went to their lockers.

"I'll see you Saturday night, right?" Darcy asked politely.

"Yes," Tegan confirmed as she smiled at him. "I'll see you at The Shaky Martini."

5:30pm on Saturday evening came by. Tegan was in her bedroom, putting on makeup, ready for her night out at The Shaky Martini. Lloyd was sitting on the bed watching her as she got ready.

"You're so beautiful," Lloyd complimented her. Tegan started to blush as she turned to face him. Even though they were seeing each other, she still felt bashful at being complimented.

"Then again, you could be covered in slime, and I'd still find you beautiful," Lloyd elaborated. Tegan looked at him, perplexed at his remark.

"Is this a hint that you're into something I don't know about?" Tegan teased him.

"No," Lloyd pointed out. "I'm just saying you're always beautiful."

"You're so cute," Tegan said as she kissed him on the lips. She went back to her mirror to finish putting on her makeup.

"So, this Darcy guy—do you reckon it'll go anywhere?" Lloyd asked inquisitively.

"I have no idea," Tegan answered honestly. "He could just see me as a colleague."

"Yes because 'just colleagues' go out on dates all the time," Lloyd sarcastically pointed out. Tegan put her makeup down.

"It's not necessarily a date. Neither of us have called it that," Tegan affirmed.

"Okay, what would you call it?" Lloyd challenged her. Tegan hesitated for a moment, not knowing how to answer that question. She faced Lloyd as she started putting her makeup away in her makeup bag.

"I don't know. Maybe I'll have more of an answer tonight," Tegan finally answered as she put her makeup bag in a cupboard. She went to Lloyd and sat on his lap.

"Are you sure you're okay with this?" Tegan asked.

"No," Lloyd answered honestly. "I don't know how I feel about all this and the idea of you being with someone else still makes me a little uneasy."

"What can I do to make it easier?" Tegan asked, keen to make Lloyd happy but maintain a happy atmosphere.

"I don't know," he answered after a moment of hesitation. Tegan started to feel uneasy in herself and got off his lap. The pleasant atmosphere between them seemed to dissipate into awkwardness.

The Shaky Martini

"I can't adjust my life to everyone else's whim. It's bad enough I'm having to be mindful of a narcissistic cokehead with a non-existent fuse. What do you want from me, Lloyd?" Tegan asked desperately.

"I don't know," Lloyd answered.

"I told you when we started this that polyamory was a part of my life. Sure, I didn't expect to meet someone else this quickly but that's the way it goes sometimes. Either you're okay with this or you're not," Tegan retorted. There was a silence between them until Tegan went to her wardrobe. She got out a dark navy flapper style dress with ornate beadings on it and a pair of tights. She placed them carefully on her bed.

"Tegan, I'm sorry. Gabriella twisted my head big time and not just with the cheating," Lloyd began to explain.

"This isn't cheating," Tegan interrupted defensively.

"I know," Lloyd replied. "I'm just saying that I can't quite help but conflate the two a little. I know this is a me problem and you haven't done anything wrong. I just need to work on it." Tegan felt he was being genuine and decided to drop the issue. She picked up the tights she was going to wear and took off her pyjama bottoms as Lloyd admired her dress.

"That is a brilliant dress," Lloyd commented.

"Thanks. I love it. I bought it for a 20s party I went to at university. It would've sucked if I only wore it once," Tegan told him.

"At least I get to see you wear it before you go," Lloyd remarked sadly. Tegan noted his sadness, feeling bad they felt he was unable to come with her.

"We'll be able to do things like this soon enough. We just need to ensure Ms Bunny Boiler simmers down or goes to prison before we can do that," Tegan told him. She put on her tights and got into her flapper dress. She started to think about the night ahead.

"*Is Lloyd really okay? Is this really a date with Darcy or are we thinking too much into it?*" As she finished getting dressed, she heard her door knock.

"Oi. Lovebirds. Put each other down. We'll be late!" Magda shouted through the door.

"Alright, give me a minute!" Tegan replied, smiling.

"That's my cue to exit," Lloyd said as he grabbed his jacket from the bedpost. "Have fun," he whispered as he started walking out of the bedroom.

It was 6:55pm and Tegan, Nadia and a fully healed Magda came up to the Shaky Martini, excited for the night ahead of them. They were all dressed to the nines in their 1920s attire. Magda was wearing a black flapper dress with a silver headband whilst Nadia was dressed in a pinstripe suit with their hair slicked back pompadour style. All three went up to the two bald bouncers dressed in all black, one of which held an electronic clipboard.

"Are you on the list?" the bouncer clutching the clipboard asked.

"Yeah I'm Magda Lawton," Magda introduced herself.

"I'm Nadia Falkner," Nadia followed.

"I'm—" Tegan started. She trailed off when she spotted Darcy coming up to her. She was struck by his confidence as he came up to her wearing a navy blue herringbone suit with a blue tie and black Oxford shoes. Something about him in the moment took her breath away. She just about managed to conceal her feelings as he made it to her. Neither were quite sure what to say to each other until Darcy silently offered her his arm. She took it, sliding her arm around his with a small smile across her face. Magda and Nadia looked on, intrigued by what was going on.

"I'm Tegan Javaman," Tegan told the bouncer with the electronic clipboard. "And this is Darcy Brandon." The bouncer looked through his list, and found them both.

"Perfect. They're waiting for you," the bouncer confirmed. He opened the door for the four of them as they entered. They went into a very large room with a gold reflective bar that had a gold top and red cushioned bar seats lined alongside it. The bottles of alcohol lit up under the lights that lit up the bar. Away from the bar was a 20s style dance floor and small tables with red chairs. The sound of heels clacking on the laminated wooden floor was accompanied by the sound of jazz band music playing on the speakers. Magda, Nadia, Tegan and Darcy were all impressed with what they saw. They stood near the bar where two bartenders waited to serve. Magda and Nadia turned to face Tegan and Darcy who unlinked their arms.

"Well Tegan," Magda started expectantly. "Aren't you going to introduce us?"

"Darcy, these are my housemates and two of my best friends, Magda and Nadia. Magda and Nadia, this is Darcy who I work with at the hospital," Tegan introduced the trio to each other in a matter of fact way.

"Lovely to meet you both," Darcy started. "You both look great."

"Thank you," Magda said.

"Where did you get your suit? I had a nightmare trying to find one that would fit me." Darcy asked Nadia. Nadia was a little taken aback but appreciative at not being questioned as to why they were wearing a suit.

"This suit belonged to my great grandfather. I had it altered to fit whilst I wore a binder," Nadia explained. "Where did you get yours?"

"Tegan and I are going to get a drink," Magda said as she linked her arm up with Tegan. "Do you two want anything?"

"I'd love a Rob Roy," Nadia requested.

"An Old Fashioned would suit me, thanks," Darcy smoothly asked.

"Okay we'll be back," Tegan said as she and Magda went to the bar.

An hour went by. There were a considerable number of people in the bar drinking cocktails and dancing. Tegan felt a sense of comfort she hadn't felt in a while as she spoke with Darcy, Jools and Georgia. The four of them were holding a cocktail apiece and enjoying the ambience as they spoke. Nadia and Magda were dancing together on the dance floor.

"This is a brilliant bar," Darcy commented. "I still remember when it first opened. The bouncers weren't so strict about ID back then."

"The previous owner was a bit laissez-faire about that sort of thing," Georgia remarked. "The new owner wanted to inject a bit of life into the place and make it respectable."

"They definitely succeeded. It looks amazing," Darcy complimented.

"Thank you," Georgia thanked him.

"So, Tegan, how's it been working back in Colton City?" Jools asked Tegan who was sipping her cocktail.

"It's pretty hectic, but it's been good. I'm getting there," Tegan replied. Darcy finished his cocktail.

"I'm going to get another drink. Anyone else want one?" Darcy asked Georgia.

"I think we're okay at the moment but thanks for asking," Georgia thanked him. Darcy headed straight back to the bar. Georgia and Jools faced Tegan. As Jools was about to say something, a bartender approached Georgia.

"Sorry Georgia," The bartender apologised. "Security are having some aggro from someone who is demanding to speak to the manager." Tegan felt a pang of fear, scared that Gabriella was going to ruin the night for her.

The Dance

♥

"It's okay. I'll be right there," Georgia said to the bartender who left. "I'll be right back." Georgia went to the entrance of The Shaky Martini where she could hear shouting. Tegan and Jools watched as they saw someone try to barge her way through the bouncers. It was an angry Gabriella. Tegan's fear was confirmed, and it created a huge amount of anxiety and guilt inside.

"Great. Tonight is ruined for sure," Tegan thought to herself. Gabriella was not deterred when she saw Georgia approach. Jools and Tegan stood together as they realised what was going on. Nadia and Magda came over to Tegan and Jools.

"Jesus why is she here?" Nadia asked, annoyed.

"Because she can. That's why," Tegan said, resigned. Darcy came back to Jools and Tegan without a drink. He stood next to Tegan, looking in the same direction as she did.

"She's back again?" Darcy asked.

"That's Gabriella for you," Tegan told him. "Either she thinks Lloyd is here or she just wants to terrorise me." Upon hearing this, Darcy instinctively held her by the shoulders. Tegan was still anxious but felt a little safer being held. Georgia reached Gabriella.

"Let me in! Don't you realise who I am?" Gabriella screamed.

"Either you leave, or I'll call the Police on you," Georgia firmly responded. Gabriella spotted Tegan with Darcy and started to lose what was left of her temper.

"That whore—I'll get you, Javaman!" Gabriella screamed at the top of her lungs, pointing at Tegan.

"I'm going to call the Police. Go away," Georgia commanded Gabriella as she stepped back and got her phone out. She dialled 999 as the bouncers tried to escort Gabriella away. Gabriella reached into her handbag and threw a couple of stink bombs at the entrance. Within seconds, a foul rotten egg smell engulfed the area as Gabriella smugly walked into the night. Guests went towards the dance floor to avoid the smell of the stink bombs. Georgia ran away from the smell, coughing and still on the phone to the Police. Jools, Nadia, Magda, Darcy, and Tegan stayed in place. Tegan's guilt intensified as the smell permeated the bar.

"God, that smell is disgusting." Jools coughed.

"I'm so sorry, Jools. I know Georgia worked so hard preparing for tonight," Tegan apologised.

"There's no need to apologise. You didn't throw the stink bombs," Jools tried to reassure her.

"But—" Tegan started.

"Tigs, you didn't do anything wrong. Accept it," Magda firmly told her. Tegan was conflicted over whether to argue or not. On the one hand, she cognitively knew she didn't do anything wrong but on the other, her heart was racked with guilt.

"I know that face; Don't even think about arguing with us," Magda reiterated. Tegan sighed, both happy for her friends' kindness but also sad for the unfolding events. Darcy took his hands away from Tegan's shoulders.

"Drink up," he told her.

"What?" Tegan asked, confused.

"I'll tell you once you've finished your drink," he instructed her. She was a little unsure, but she proceeded to drink up until her glass was empty.

"Good," said Darcy. "Now come with me." He held his hand out to Tegan. She hesitated for a moment before taking his hand and handing her empty glass to Magda. They walked to the dance floor together as Nadia, Magda and Jools watched on. Tegan was confused as to what Darcy was up to. They stopped at the edge of the dancefloor where music continued to play.

"What are you doing?" Tegan asked him. They went on to the dancefloor together. Darcy separated his hand from hers and faced her.

"Tegan, would you do me the honour of dancing with me?" Darcy asked politely. Tegan was perplexed by this request. She wasn't sure what this had to do with anything that just unfolded. She wasn't sure what to say to him until she saw his smile. The smile that could melt the iciest of characters. He was up to something for sure, but she didn't care. She couldn't resist him as she stepped on to the dance floor with him. He had one hand around her waist, she had a hand on his shoulder and their free hands held each other. They began to dance together in perfect time with the music. As they continued to move together, Tegan started to smile.

"See? You're cheering up already," Darcy commented. This only made her smile more as she realised what he was trying to do. Nadia, Jools and Magda watched on with great interest.

"There's something about him I can't quite place," Jools commented as she fidgeted by tapping her glass.

"He's a bit of a smooth operator," Nadia continued.

"Look at her; she's smiling," Magda argued.

"And?" Nadia asked.

"Have you seen her smile like that since all this nonsense with Lloyd and Gabriella began? Hell, did she ever smile like that when she was with Felicity?" Magda pointed out. Nadia and Jools looked at Tegan and Darcy again.

"I guess you're right." Nadia conceded with a smile across their face.

The following Friday morning dawned over the residents of Colton City. The sun shone brightly in the May sky as Tegan got up from her bed, ready to tackle the day ahead of her. She felt oddly optimistic as she went into the bathroom and put some deodorant on her armpits. As she left the bathroom to get changed in her bedroom, she encountered Magda, dressed in her dressing gown.

"Magda! I thought you had work today," Tegan asked her, surprised.

"I have today off. You?" Magda answered nonchalantly.

"I'm at work today then I'm going to try and visit Sara. It feels like every day is a work day at the moment," Tegan joked with her.

"At least you have Dr Dishy to swoon over," Magda teased her. Tegan felt incredibly self-conscious at that moment. She felt almost called out by Magda.

"I have absolutely no idea what you're on about," Tegan lied as she started to blush.

"C'mon Tigs, you're a terrible liar," Magda countered. "You're so into him and I think he might be into you as well."

"I better not be late." Tegan brushed off Magda as she blushed. She rushed into her bedroom and started getting dressed into her work uniform. Thoughts rushed through her head. Did he feel anything beyond friendship? Was too much being read into things? Was backing away the best option before feelings got hurt? She didn't have a lot of time to ruminate as she grabbed her large handbag and shoes. She raced down the stairs and put her shoes on. Magda sat at the top of the stairs.

"I didn't mean to embarrass you just now. I'm sorry," Magda apologised.

"It's cool," Tegan dismissed as she started putting her shoes on. "I'll live."

"Tegan, not dealing with your emotions might be what makes us autistics great but it's not healthy. At some point, you're going to have to confront your feelings," Magda warned her. Tegan turned to face her, flustered and irritated.

"You're almost as bad as Sara. You'd think having a baby would make her less invested in her little sister's love life but apparently not," Tegan complained.

"She wants you to be happy just like the rest of us," Magda argued as she stood up from the stairs. "Is that so wrong?"

"No." Tegan sighed. "But please let me do this on my own timeline."

"Okay. Just don't dawdle. He might lose interest," Magda explained. Tegan smiled at her briefly as she started to head out the door.

"Have you had breakfast?" Magda shouted as Tegan opened the door.

"I'll get some on the way," Tegan shouted back as she left the house.

Forced Proximity

♥

I t was lunch time for Tegan, but she was struggling to eat her sandwich in the staff room. She ate half of it then stopped when she received a text from Lloyd that read "Do you want to meet after work?" Suddenly, she looked at the rest of her sandwich and started to feel nauseous. It wasn't the fact that Lloyd had texted her that made her feel queasy; it was the idea of facing up to her feelings about both the men in her life. After all, to her, there was every chance Darcy didn't like her back and Lloyd resented her polyamory. All that swept away the instant Sinead entered the staff room in a hurry.

"Tegan! Thank goodness," Sinead started.

"Are you okay, Sinead?" Tegan asked, concerned.

"Yes. Dr Brandon has to head up to a complicated birth with Dr Birch in the ICU. They want a midwife to accompany them. I wouldn't ask but the others are all busy, we're short staffed, and I've got to pick my daughter up from school. Can you head up with them?" Sinead asked. Tegan hesitated for a moment but decided to push her feelings aside for the sake of her work.

"Sure. I'll put this sandwich in the fridge and head right up," Tegan answered.

"You're a star. Thanks!" Sinead said as Tegan placed the rest of her sandwich in the fridge. Sinead quickly left the room and Tegan followed behind her. She wandered through the maternity ward towards the exit. Darcy was waiting for her at the exit leading to the rest of the hospital. Tegan's heart raced upon seeing him, but she continued as if everything was normal.

"Great. Let's get going," Darcy greeted her as he held the door open for her. They walked through the door together and headed for a lift.

"What's the situation?" Tegan asked.

"Forty week old woman in labour who was in a major RTC about an hour ago. Baby is in distress," Darcy explained.

"Forgive me for asking but if you and Dr Birch are there, why do you need me?" Tegan enquired.

"We want the baby out sooner rather than later. We felt for now a midwife-led delivery would be the best option for the baby," Darcy answered.

"Right," Tegan agreed. They got into the staff lift that would take them to the right floor. Darcy pressed the button for the third floor but a few seconds into their journey, the lift suddenly jolted and stopped. Tegan and Darcy looked at each other, confused and concerned. Darcy pressed the button for the third floor again, but the lift didn't move. Tegan's face fell as she realised they were trapped. Darcy kept pushing the button for the third floor.

"Darcy, we're stuck," Tegan said with an unmistaken sense of panic in her voice. "We better press the alarm button." Darcy stopped pushing the third floor button and pressed the alarm button. It let off a brief yet loud alarm which distressed them both.

"How can I help you?" a crackled voice over the intercom bellowed.

"We're stuck in the staff lift near the Maternity department and there's a patient who needs our help. Can you get us out?" Darcy asked as politely as he could muster.

"We'll get on it," the voice replied nonchalantly. Darcy and Tegan looked at each other with a sense of dread. They were stuck. Darcy turned back to the intercom speaker, uncharacteristically annoyed.

"I don't want to be pushy but, as I said earlier, we have a patient in critical condition that needs help," Darcy explained.

"Well, they'll have to find someone else," the voice responded unconcerned. "Just sit tight and you'll be out." Darcy, appalled at the lack of concern, gave up and faced Tegan who was very apprehensive.

"I guess we're stuck here for a while," Darcy said, defeated. Tegan got her phone out. She had minimal signal.

"I have a little signal. I could see if Sinead has gone?" Tegan offered. Darcy got out his phone which had no signal.

"I've not got any signal. Ask Sinead to speak to Dr Birch," Darcy requested. Tegan started to call Sinead and wandered to the intercom. She was about to speak again when she noticed the specifications nearby. She looked up the information of the lift company and sighed with a sense of resignation; it was owned by Stanford Ltd.

"Shit." Tegan cursed.

"What is it?" Darcy asked. Tegan handed her phone over to Darcy and sat in a corner of the lift, trying her level best not to cry. Darcy was about to go comfort her when he heard Sinead answer Tegan's phone.

"Sinead, it's me. Tegan and I are stranded in a lift. I need you to let Dr Birch know," Darcy explained.

"What? Is that you Darcy?" Sinead could be heard saying on the other end.

"Yes, it's me. Tegan and I are stranded in a lift. Please let Dr Birch know," Darcy said again.

"I will. Text me if you need anything else. Your signal is really bad," Sinead said as she hung up. Darcy locked the phone and tried to hand it to Tegan who had her head in her hands. He put the phone on the floor and sat next to her.

"Is there something you want to tell me?" Darcy asked calmly. Tegan faced him, sadly.

"The lift is run by Stanford Ltd. The CEO of which is Nathaniel Stanford, Gabriella's father," she told him, still trying her best not to cry.

"I'm sure the lifts aren't run by them," Darcy tried to reassure her.

"Gabriella's Dad is a wealthy multi-entrepreneur who treats his daughter like a Princess. If she wants something, he gets it for her. If she wants to bribe a worker to keep someone she doesn't like trapped in a lift for whatever reason, she can do so," Tegan refuted.

"That woman is deranged," Darcy remarked. "What if we had a critical patient with us?"

"She doesn't care," Tegan commented in a morose manner. "I think the ends justify the means for Gabriella."

"Why haven't the Police arrested her yet?" Darcy pondered, irritated at the situation.

"Your guess is as good as mine," Tegan speculated. "I wouldn't be surprised if Daddy knows the right people in the right places to keep her out of jail for now."

Lloyd was at home sending a text to Tegan. He chilled out in his bedroom where the walls were covered in band posters. He was sitting on his double bed, relaxing to the sound of Feeder's 'Echo Park' album playing on his phone. He felt relaxed for the first time in quite a while. For once, he didn't think about Gabriella or the drama that she had caused for the past few weeks. He heard a knock on his bedroom door.

He paused the music and opened the door. It was his father who was holding a jacket.

"I'm going out with some of my friends. Do you want to come with us?"

"Thanks Dad, but I'll be seeing Tegan after she finishes work."

"How is that going?" Lloyd's Dad asked.

"It's fine, thanks," Lloyd said.

"I'm sure it would be better without your ex in the picture," his Dad pointed out.

"Yes, Dad," Lloyd agreed.

"Keep yourself safe, son. I love you."

"I love you too," Lloyd said to his Dad as he walked away. He shut the door and put his music back on. For the next half an hour, he scrolled on social media and listened to the music in peace. Suddenly, a small stone was thrown at his window. He looked at the window but didn't get up to see who threw that stone. Deciding to ignore it, he went back to his scrolling. A second later, a second stone was thrown at his window which cracked it. Annoyed, Lloyd paused his music and got up from his bed. He went to his window and looked at who was throwing the stones at his window; Gabriella. Angry, he impulsively rushed out of his room, down the stairs and to his front door. He opened it and spotted Gabriella approaching him.

Pregnant With Disaster

♥

"Go away," Lloyd told her firmly as she stepped in front of him.

"Lloyd, we need to—" Gabriella tried to start.

"No. The only time I want to see you is when you're in court over everything you've done to Tegan and her friends," Lloyd interrupted. He was about to shut the door when she quickly stopped him.

"Lloyd, please, I need to talk to you," Gabriella pleaded as she stepped into the house.

"You have nothing you could possibly say to me that I'd want to hear," Lloyd told her as he tried to guide her out of his house.

"I'm pregnant!" Gabriella screamed.

Trapped in the lift, Tegan and Darcy sat across from each other in an awkward and tense silence. Tegan's phone was now in her work tunic. They seemed unable to say anything to each other. Tegan fiddled with her tunic out of anxiety. Darcy looked at her and felt bad for her predicament. He became keen to keep her mind off of what was going on. He thought for a moment.

"Did you know that Platypuses sweat milk?" he started. Tegan stopped fidgeting to look at him, intrigued.

"I thought they were aquatic and didn't have teats? Surely they need teats to produce milk," Tegan argued, briefly gesturing over her breasts before stopping out of embarrassment.

"That's true," Darcy explained. "The milk just oozes from the surface of their skin."

"Ah. That's bizarre," Tegan said.

"Yeah but interesting, right?" Darcy replied.

"Yeah," Tegan agreed. Darcy smiled at her, trying to cheer her up. She smiled a little back.

"Did you know that the Pope can't be an organ donor?" Tegan told Darcy.

"Is it because he's old?" Darcy wondered.

"No. It's because once he dies, his body belongs to the Church and must be buried intact according to the Catholic faith," Tegan explained.

"Huh," said Darcy as he took in the information. A brief silence befell the pair as they tried to conjure up more random facts to tell each other.

"Venus is the only planet to spin clockwise," Darcy told Tegan.

"The proper name for a hashtag is an octothorpe," said Tegan.

"The circulatory system is more than 60,000 miles long."

"There were active volcanoes on the moon during the time of the dinosaurs."

"Feeling a little better?" Darcy asked happily.

"A very little," Tegan admitted. "But what I'd like to know more about is you."

"Me? I'm not that interesting a person," Darcy tried to put her off.

"I'd argue otherwise. Besides, it looks as if we could be here for a while. We may as well get to know each other a bit more," Tegan suggested. Darcy didn't feel able to argue with her logic.

"Okay but only if I get to ask you questions too," Darcy insisted.

"If you insist." Tegan smiled.

Lloyd looked at Gabriella, stunned. He wasn't sure whether to believe her or not. After all, it wouldn't be the first time she'd lied to him about something. By the same token, she'd never lied about something as important as pregnancy to him. Could she really be believed? Gabriella pounced on his hesitation, sensing weakness in his resolve.

"Baby, I know you still love me. You don't want our child to grow up in a broken home, do you?" Gabriella insisted.

"How do I know you're telling the truth?" Lloyd questioned her. Gabriella reached into her purse and drew out a picture of an ultrasound. She threw it at him.

"Happy now?" Gabriella sniped. Lloyd picked up the ultrasound picture. He looked at it in amazement. He was staring at an image that might've contained his child. He took it in for a moment before remembering who he was dealing with.

"This isn't another trick, is it?" Lloyd queried sceptically. Gabriella snatched the ultrasound picture from Lloyd's hands.

"Why don't you believe me?" Gabriella screamed at him. She turned away from him and started to cry in a histrionic nature. Lloyd, torn between believing her or not, placed his hand on her shoulder, not wishing for her to cry.

"Please don't cry. We can figure this out," Lloyd comforted her. Gabriella turned to face him with a gleam of expectation in her eyes.

"Really?" she said, hopeful.

"First of all, you need to cut out your campaign of harassment on Tegan. She didn't do anything wrong," he told her unyieldingly.

"But she—" she tried to start indignantly.

"But nothing. We won't be able to even begin contemplating the next step in co-parenting if you're going to continue harassing an innocent person," Lloyd firmly interrupted.

"When you say the next step, what do you mean? Could we make this work?" Gabriella deflected. Lloyd put his head down, conflicted. He didn't fully believe her, but he didn't want to end up as some kind of deadbeat. Gabriella approached Lloyd.

"I want this to work, Lloyd. I don't want to raise our child in a broken home," Gabriella continued, stroking his cheek. Lloyd didn't want to give in to her. He wanted to keep his agreement to Tegan, but he just couldn't resist her at that moment. He held her hand and began to kiss her.

Meanwhile in the lift, Tegan and Darcy were still trapped but their anxieties over it seemed to dissipate as they kept talking to each other. Their comfort around each other intensified with every passing minute.

"Okay, what do you want to know?" Darcy coolly asked.

"About what?" Tegan enquired. Darcy gave her a knowing look until she put two and two together; he was inviting her to ask questions about him. Tegan thought about it for a moment. There was quite a bit she wanted to know, and their current predicament felt like the best time to ask questions. After all, they had a captive audience in each other: why not utilise it?

Once More, With

Passion

♥

"What's your favourite colour?" Tegan eventually asked.

"Yellow. If you could go on holiday right now, where would you go?" Darcy replied.

"Valletta in Malta. I've been once before and it's just beautiful. Even some of the roundabouts nearby are beautiful," Tegan responded. "What's your favourite food?"

"Thai food. I especially enjoy Chicken Pad Thai. Did you enjoy school?"

"No. I did fine academically but I got bullied a lot. Do you have any pets?"

"Yes, a cat named Heathcliff. How did you decide to practise polyamory?"

"I was never keen on monogamy. It just didn't seem to make a lot of sense. How about you?"

"My ex-boyfriend and ex-girlfriend wanted me to try it. It has worked well for me so far." A silence briefly fell between the two as

Darcy struggled to think of what to ask Tegan. He fiddled with his hands as he thought.

"How old are you? How many siblings do you have?" Tegan asked randomly. The randomness of it threw Darcy enough for him to stop fiddling with his hands but he kept his composure.

"I'm 35 and I just have my younger sister Beth. Yourself?" he told her.

"I'm 25 and I have Sara as my older sister, my two teenage half-brothers and my step brother," she answered.

"Your parents aren't together?" Darcy opined. Tegan shuffled a little uncomfortably and started fiddling with her work tunic in a stimming manner. She focussed her gaze on her hands.

"Yeah. My Dad died when I was 10 due to cancer," Tegan said sadly.

"I'm sorry," he apologised. Tegan looked up to see his genuine remorse on his face.

"It's okay. It was a long time ago," said Tegan. "What about your parents? There's quite an age gap between you and Beth." Darcy looked down at the floor before facing Tegan again and took a deep breath.

"I didn't know my Dad. I don't think my Mum really knew him that well. I can't ask her—" He hesitated, trying to figure out the right words to let Tegan know the full answer.

"Beth's Dad murdered my Mum whilst I was in medical school," Darcy finally admitted. Tegan's heart dropped at that information. The guilt over asking that question and the empathy for his position consumed her heart. She moved herself next to Darcy and impulsively placed her hand on his, just craving to comfort him.

"None of Beth's Dad's family wanted her and my Mum was an only child. It was either me or foster care. She's my sister and I couldn't abandon her," Darcy elaborated.

"I can't imagine it's been smooth sailing," Tegan remarked softly.

"Juggling my medical training whilst taking care of a young child wasn't easy but I couldn't give up. She's a great kid. I don't regret it," Darcy continued. He held her hand tightly. He faced her and they smiled briefly at each other. They looked away from each other, unsure of what to do or what the other person was thinking. In spite of the romantic tension building between them with every passing second, they were both unsure of the other person's intent. They turned to face each other again, still holding hands.

"We're holding hands," Tegan stated.

"I know," said Darcy. Their hearts raced as they inched closer to each other. They hesitated for a moment as their lips touched but, a second later, they kissed tenderly. They both felt a rush as they finally locked lips. Their kiss became more passionate as their pent up feelings flowed out of them. Their hands remained held together as they continued their romantic embrace. They both got lost in the moment, enjoying every second of it. Suddenly, the lift jolted down. The duo stopped kissing and holding hands. They quickly stood up as the lift slowly went down to the ground floor. Tegan stepped away from Darcy as they composed themselves. The lift doors opened to two irritated maintenance workers looking in. Tegan focussed her attention on the situation at hand.

"Where have you been? We were on our way to a critical patient," Tegan angrily told the maintenance workers who shrugged at her curt comment.

"It's alright Tegan, let's just take the stairs," Darcy told her. He and Tegan rushed away from the scene together, both keen to focus on the problem at hand.

Lloyd and Gabriella continued to kiss each other passionately. Gabriella's hands started to wander away from his face, down his torso and to the belt of his jeans. He tried to pull away, but she pulled him back to her. He pushed her away, realising what he was doing. A wave of guilt and shame waved through him.

"You want me," Gabriella boasted.

"Is that all this was—proving you can get what you want?" Lloyd said indignantly.

"Why deny yourself when you know you want this?" Gabriella smirked, pointing at her slender body in a bragging manner. This disgusted Lloyd.

"I'm not going back to you," Lloyd said firmly. Gabriella's smirking expression fell into a face of anger.

"You're making a big mistake!" Gabriella screamed at him.

"The mistake I made was believing your crap," Lloyd countered as calmly as possible in spite of his anger.

"What about our baby? Do you really want it to be a bastard?" Gabriella cruelly snarked, holding her flat tummy.

"Good luck with that. I'm not doing anything without a DNA test," Lloyd explained. Gabriella went to strike Lloyd, but he held her wrist tightly. She used the opportunity to punch him with her other hand when he wasn't prepared. The strike caused him to let go of her. The escalation in violence shocked him: he had been slapped and scratched before, but he didn't expect to be punched. She tried to hit him again, but he pushed her away. She spat on him which landed on his face. He wiped it away in disgust.

"You'll pay for this!" Gabriella yelled as she left the house. Lloyd turned his back to her as she left. Once he heard the door slam, his composure melted away. The guilt and anger he felt washed over him like a shower from the depths of Hell. He thought he was beyond her manipulation tactics and felt appalling for falling for something so transparent. He promised Tegan he wouldn't touch Gabriella again. He felt a great amount of shame for even letting Gabriella in, let alone kissing her. He despaired at the idea of losing Tegan, but he knew he had to do the right thing and tell her what he did. He got out his phone and started calling Tegan, but it went to voicemail.

"Ah yeah, she's at work," he remembered. "I'll talk to her once she's finished."

It was 10pm, and Tegan was in the staff room drinking a cup of tea. She was trying to process the events of the day but couldn't stop thinking about the kiss she had with Darcy in the lift. It was exhilarating, passionate, and everything she hoped it would be, yet she couldn't shake off an anxious feeling that came with the uncertainty of where to go from there. She couldn't figure out if the kiss was a fluke of the moment or the start of something more. She didn't have much longer to reflect as one of the receptionists came into the staff room.

"Hey Tegan," the receptionist greeted her. "There's someone to see you." Tegan felt dread as she heard those words.

"Is it a man or a woman?" Tegan asked anxiously.

"A man. Shall I tell him to come through?" the receptionist offered. Tegan felt a little relieved but still unsure as to what was going on.

"No. I'll come to him. Thanks." The receptionist left, leaving Tegan to finish her cup of tea quickly. Tegan swilled the cup of debris and placed it in the sink.

Code Black

♥

S he grabbed her large hand bag and walked slowly to the reception area. She was relieved to see Lloyd waiting for her.

"I thought I missed you," Lloyd greeted as he hugged her. They came apart from each other. There was an awkward tension between the two as they stood apart.

"I did a little overtime. I got trapped in one of your ex's Dad's lifts earlier," Tegan told him. Lloyd sunk his head briefly before raising it back up again.

"You must be exhausted. Let's get you home," Lloyd declared. They left the Reception area through the public exit. By now it was pitch black with the exception of the starlight in the sky and a few broken street lamps.

"They should really fix those," Tegan pointed at the street lamps.

"Good luck telling the council that," Lloyd told her sardonically. They approached Lloyd's blue hatchback car. As Lloyd went to get his keys from his pocket, a pink car parked opposite turned their lights on. They drove straight to Lloyd's car. Tegan and Lloyd quickly jumped out of the way in opposite directions to get away from the incoming car. The car crashed gently into Lloyd's. Tegan and Lloyd faced each other briefly before facing the emerging driver: Gabriella. She was holding a phone in one hand whilst keeping the other hand in her pocket.

"Get your hands off my boyfriend!" Gabriella screeched at Tegan as she approached her.

"Last I checked, he dumped you," Tegan responded in an irritable manner. She was not in the mood to deal with Gabriella's nonsense again. Lloyd came around to their side of the crashed cars to see what was going on.

"Is that so?" Gabriella challenged Tegan. Lloyd almost got to Tegan's side when he was stopped by the back passenger of Gabriella's car: a man he didn't know. The man grabbed Lloyd and held him back.

"What is going on, Gabriella?" Lloyd shouted as he struggled with the man. Gabriella coolly turned to face him.

"You're so blinded by her witchcraft that you don't even get it," Gabriella scolded him. She faced Tegan again.

"You think you're so hot. He's mine, you whore!" Gabriella yelled at Tegan, who lost all patience with the shenanigans.

"Oh no: Gabriella is here with her followers! What are you going to do—keep yelling crap again to your Instagram followers? I'm so scared," Tegan mocked her. Gabriella took her concealed hand out of her pocket to reveal a serrated kitchen knife. Tegan's mocking tone disappeared, and she started to feel a sense of panic, not knowing how far Gabriella was going to take the feud. She froze in place out of fear. Lloyd saw the knife as well and fought even harder to escape the grip of the burly man restraining him but to no avail.

"Gabriella, put the knife down," Lloyd pleaded.

"It's too late for that, Lloyd. Tegan here decided to mess with me. Now I get my revenge!" Gabriella declared.

"What—as if sending fake nudes, setting your followers on me, harassing me at work, harassing my sister to the point of early labour, and nearly killing Magda wasn't enough?" Tegan questioned her.

"It's not enough until you're gone, Javaman," Gabriella screamed in her face, tightening her grip on the knife. Tegan turned behind her to realise there was a wall blocking her from a clear escape. Gabriella lost her cool: she put her phone in her pocket. She grabbed Tegan's hair with her free hand and forced her to face Lloyd.

"You know, I saw Lloyd earlier and we had a little reunion. We're going to have a baby together," Gabriella said cruelly in Tegan's ear. Tegan looked to Lloyd who stopped trying to escape. His face dropped as the revelation came to light. Tegan was confused, scared and hurt by what she had heard.

"Is it true?" Tegan asked, in shock.

"Tegan—" Lloyd started softly.

"Yes. We're going to be one happy family. Something you'll never get," Gabriella interrupted in a boastful manner. Tegan desperately tried to escape but Gabriella's grip was too strong. She held the knife high and suddenly thrust it deep into Tegan's lower abdomen.

"Tegan!" Lloyd yelled. Tegan couldn't fully react for a moment out of shock. She snapped out of it once she saw the knife deep inside of her. Gabriella coldly pushed Tegan to the ground. The pain in Tegan's side started to kick in as she fell. The sensation of the knife was like a violent punch to the abdomen. Gabriella faced Lloyd happily.

"Now, my love, it's time for us to start our lives together," Gabriella stated.

"I wouldn't be with you if you were the last woman alive," Lloyd declared. Gabriella's rage boiled over once again. She went back to Tegan who was trying to get up.

"I heard that once you've been stabbed, one of the worst things to do is to remove the knife from the stab wound without medical care." Gabriella smirked as she removed the knife from Tegan's lower abdomen. Gabriella quickly got up and went to Lloyd.

"Shame. You had such a pretty voice," Gabriella coolly remarked. Without warning, she stabbed him in the front of his neck near his throat. She removed the knife from his neck, went to Tegan and stabbed her again on the other side of her lower abdomen. Her accomplice let Lloyd fall to the ground and he & Gabriella ran away together as she removed the knife from Tegan's abdomen. Once she was sure they were gone, a pale Tegan got onto her front and started crawling towards Lloyd despite her own situation. Lloyd was bleeding from his neck catastrophically. He tried to speak but it came out as a bloody gargle.

"Don't talk. Put some pressure on your neck," Tegan told him as she inched closer to him. He weakly placed one of his hands on one side of his neck wound but struggled to maintain pressure. The blood from Tegan's abdominal wounds were bleeding profusely, leaving a trail of blood behind her. She took out her mobile phone from her pocket. As she started to dial a number, she started to feel incredibly dizzy and cold as she fought a losing battle for consciousness.

Magda was relaxing in the living room at the home she shared with Nadia and Tegan. She was in her pyjamas, watching television and drinking a glass of wine. She checked her phone: it was 10:05 pm.

"Huh," Magda thought to herself. "It's kind of late." She turned her attention back to watching the television when suddenly, her phone went off: Tegan was calling her. Curious and a little concerned, Magda answered the phone.

"Tegan! What's up?" Magda began.

"Magda! I need you to get help. Gabriella has stabbed us," Tegan interrupted, trying her best to maintain calm. Those words hit Magda as if she were hit by a speeding train: whilst she feared this outcome, she never expected it.

"What?" Magda squealed with tears welling in her eyes.

"We've not got a lot of time. Call 999 and tell them there are two people stabbed by the side of two crashed cars in the carpark of the maternity unit at Colton City hospital," Tegan told her quickly on the other side of the phone. Magda started to cry silently, trying but failing to maintain her composure.

"Tigs—"

"Mags, we can't wait and it hurts to scream. Hang up and get help," Tegan told her. Magda panicked for a brief moment before snapping into action. She hung up the phone and called 999. As she relayed the information to the operator on the other side of the phone, Nadia came into the room in their pyjamas. They were confused as to what was going on and why Magda was crying on the phone. After Magda was done on the phone, she turned to face Nadia who was standing there concerned with their arms crossed.

"Nadia. It's Code Black," Magda said as she brushed past them and rushed up the stairs to her bedroom.

The Morning After

♥

Forty-five minutes later Magda and Nadia, now dressed in proper clothes, rushed to the entrance of the Accident & Emergency department at Colton City Hospital. Their panic and fright were spread across their face as they ran into Sara who was hanging up her phone. Sara spotted Magda and Nadia and prepared to talk to them.

"Magda. Nadia. Good to see you both," Sara greeted them, exhausted and anxious herself.

"Sara. How is she?" Magda asked frantically. Sara paused for a moment to compose herself in order to get the message across.

"They're in surgery with her now. Thankfully one of the stab wounds missed her major organs but they think the other hit a couple of her organs so they're operating on her now," Sara told them.

"Did they say whether she—" Nadia started. They found themself unable to continue that sentence. The idea of it was too much for them. Magda placed a friendly hand on their shoulder, sharing in their fears.

"They're not sure. It could go either way," Sara explained solemnly. There was a moment where the gravity of what was going on sank in for Nadia, Sara and Magda.

"How about Lloyd? Is he okay?" Nadia asked innocently. Sara's head sunk for a moment before she raised it again, trying her best not to cry.

"I ran into his Dad in the relatives room. There wasn't anything they could do to save him. He lost far too much blood, and the injury was catastrophic," Sara responded. The trio was silent for a moment as the weight of the information sunk into their minds. Magda took her hand off of Nadia's shoulder.

"Is your Mum on her way?" Magda enquired.

"She is. How about Jools and Georgia?" Sara replied.

"We couldn't get a hold of them, so I texted them. We had a code for any sort of crisis like this after Magda's hospitalisation. I'm sure at least one of them will be here in the morning," Nadia answered.

"How're you holding up?" Magda questioned Sara. Sara thought about it for a moment before she answered.

"It's weird. I should be happily looking after my newborn son but instead I'm facing the prospect of losing my sister," Sara admitted with a heavy sigh as she crossed her arms.

"Do you need any help? We can always wait for your Mum if you want to go home," Nadia said to Sara.

"I'm okay. I'd rather be here but thank you," Sara thanked them.

Whilst the sun rose on the outside, the feeling within Magda was sombre as she sat alone in the hospital cafeteria nursing a cup of coffee. Her sleep deprived face showed her exhaustion as she sipped her drink. She got out her phone to check the time: it was 5:15 am. She sighed as she saw no notifications for any messages. There were a surprising amount of people nearby, but she hardly processed their existence. Nadia approached her with a cup of coffee of their own.

"Are you sure you should be having another coffee?" Nadia asked as they sat opposite her.

"I haven't taken my ADHD meds and frankly, I'd prefer some coffee," Magda answered as she fiddled with her coffee cup. "Did you speak to Tegan's boss?"

"I didn't need to. She already knew: the Police got to her first," Nadia told her.

"So, the Police actually bothered to show up and do something? That's nice," Magda remarked sarcastically.

"I know," Nadia said in a resigned manner.

"They could've prevented this if they'd bothered to lock Gabriella up for everything else she'd done," Magda said angrily. "You'd have thought my peanut encounter would've been enough."

"I wouldn't be surprised if Daddy found a way to delay the process," Nadia responded calmly.

"She has been pretty quick in her escalation too. How long has it been—a couple of weeks?"

"It's been a few weeks since Lloyd broke up with Gabriella. It feels a lot longer than that."

"I know, right? So much has happened."

"Tell me about it," a female voice joined in. Magda and Nadia turned to face her: it was Georgia who was holding a cup of tea.

"Georgia!" Magda greeted her.

"Isn't this a bit late for you to be awake?" Magda asked her as Georgia sat down between her and Nadia.

"I finished my shift a couple of hours ago, got changed at home then came straight over," Georgia answered. "Jools is still asleep. She's got Carla to look after."

"Thank you for coming," Magda thanked her.

"I'm sorry I couldn't get here sooner. How is she?" Georgia queried.

"We don't know. She's still in surgery. Sara is going to let us know either way," Magda answered. Georgia took a sip from her cup of tea. An awkward silence befell the trio as they struggled to think of what to say to each other. Magda was frightened of this scenario happening, but she didn't think it would likely happen until today. There she was, hoping against all hope her best friend would survive.

"How was your shift?" Nadia asked out of the blue. Magda appreciated the opportunity to think about something else.

"Oh, your usual Friday night at a cocktail bar: lots of drunk posh people who think they're above it until they puke up their zillion cocktails up on the floor," Georgia replied casually.

"That night at the opening party was fun excluding the stink bombs," Magda reminisced happily.

"It was nice to see Tegan have a good time for once," Georgia chimed in.

"Darcy certainly knew how to cheer her up," Nadia remarked.

"Has anyone told him what's happened?" Georgia enquired. Magda faced Nadia and her face fell as the realisation hit.

"Oh—" Magda began.

"It's okay, Magda: when I spoke to Tegan's boss, I asked her to tell him. She's going to tell Darcy in a more sociable hour," Nadia interrupted.

"Thank goodness. He needs to know. I think he'd want to be here," Magda said, a little relieved. A message came up on Magda's phone. She read it. Her expression changed as she faced Nadia and Georgia.

"What is it, Mags?" Georgia asked.

"It's Sara. She's asked us to come to the relatives room."

It had just gone 9am. Nadia was sitting in the quiet and calm relatives room in the Intensive Care Unit. The ticking of the clock was all that could be heard. They were waiting awkwardly in silence, unsure what to say to each other until Magda, Jools, and Georgia came through the door.

"Hey all," Jools greeted the pair.

"Hey. Is Carla okay?" Nadia asked.

"Yeah. She's with my sister and her kids today. I figured she wouldn't enjoy being in the hospital for hours on end no matter how much she likes Auntie Tegan," Jools confirmed.

"That's fair enough," said Nadia. Sara came through the door right behind Magda, Jools and Georgia. Nadia stood up whilst Magda, Jools and Georgia turned to face Sara. There was a moment of silence before Sara spoke.

"Sorry for keeping you waiting," Sara apologised. The other four waited with bated breath for more information.

A Citizen's Arrest

♥

"The operation was pretty intense and not smooth sailing. She lost a lot of blood, and she lost not only a lot of blood but an ovary too. She's in a serious but stable condition. She should survive but it'll take some time," Sara told the group. A wave of repose flooded the room as Magda, Nadia, Jools & Georgia reacted to the news. Nadia felt a wave of relief they hadn't felt all night, relieved their friend was going to survive. They uncharacteristically initiated a hug with Magda before letting go and composing themself.

"When can we see her?" Georgia asked enthusiastically.

"You can see her but she's still asleep. She probably won't wake up for a while. Mum's with her for now," Sara answered.

"We could always go back to the cafeteria for a while. Could you let us know when she's awake?" Nadia proposed to Sara.

"That's fine. I'll let you know," Sara agreed. Sara, Magda, Nadia, Jools and Georgia left the relatives room and started walking down the corridor when they were met with Darcy who was rushing towards them. His demeanour was far away from his usual, cool manner: he looked bereft and scared.

"Thank goodness it's you lot," Darcy started. "How is she? Is she okay?" Nadia stepped forward.

"She's going to be okay, but her injuries were pretty bad. Her Mum is still with her," Nadia told him. The relief on his face was clear for the group to see as a tear went down his face.

"We're going to the cafeteria if you want to come join us?" Magda offered.

"Okay," he agreed.

Darcy, Georgia, Jools, Magda, Nadia and Sara sat together at a large table in the cafeteria, holding drinks. Darcy tapped on his coffee cup out of anxiety as the group sat together in silence. Sara turned to him.

"I'm sorry, I don't think we've ever met before," Sara spoke up.

"Oh. I'm Darcy. I work with your sister," Darcy told her.

"Oh so you're Darcy. She's talked about you before," Sara explained. Darcy perked up a little.

"In what way?" Darcy asked innocently. Sara hesitated to answer. Magda, Georgia, Jools and Nadia shuffled a little awkwardly, which didn't go unnoticed by Darcy. As he was about to say something, Nadia faced him.

"Oh for crying out loud," Nadia exclaimed. "Do you like her, Darcy?" Darcy felt very on the spot with the question whilst the others sighed.

"Like her?" he wondered.

"Do you fancy her or are you leading her on?" Nadia asked bluntly.

"Nadia!" Magda reprimanded them.

"Actually, I'm with Nadia. We saw you together at The Shaky Martini and we know you both get on pretty well at work. What's the end game?" Georgia joined in. Darcy took a deep breath: he would've preferred to have spoken to Tegan about his feelings for her but he felt as if he couldn't escape the scrutiny.

"I really like her. She's sweet, she's hard working, and she's beautiful. I think about her all the time: the way she moves, the way she flicks her hair, and the way she smells," Darcy confessed as he thought of her. "She's a wonderful woman. I'm happy just to know her but I would be even happier if we were more." Everyone else at the table paid attention with such raptured awe that they almost didn't register he'd stopped talking.

"Why haven't you told her this?" Jools asked.

"I didn't want to overpush any boundaries by being selfish," Darcy admitted. "I felt like she had enough going on with Lloyd & Gabriella for me to push myself into her life." A silence fell among the group as Darcy took a sip out of his coffee as the reality of the situation gripped everyone. He felt a guilty sense of relief mixed with concern about how Tegan was going to be.

"I'm going to go upstairs," Sara said as she stood up. "I'll let you all know when Tegan is awake and ready for visitors."

A few hours went by slowly. Tegan was lying in the Intensive Care Unit, dressed in a white & blue hospital gown and wearing an oxygen mask on her face. She was connected to a number of beeping monitors that observed her vital signs. There were a few other patients in the surrounding bays being treated as she slept by various nurses and doctors. Tegan was still recovering from her medically induced sleep, hardly able to comprehend what was going on around her. As she was beginning to get her bearings, a woman dressed in a police uniform wearing a GoPro camera approached Tegan. She had a pair of handcuffs in her right hand.

"Tegan Javaman?" the woman asked. Tegan, who was still processing what was going on, didn't answer her.

"I'm performing a citizen's arrest," the woman declared as she started cuffing a defenceless Tegan's hands together. A nurse noticed what was going on and stopped the woman from attempting to pick up Tegan. At that moment, Sara came into the bay and helped the nurse overpower the woman with the GoPro.

"What the hell are you doing?" Sara asked as she restrained the woman. Another nurse who came to help pressed the panic button near Tegan's bed.

"This is for Lloyd's death. She's responsible!" the woman screamed. It was like a record scratch in Tegan's head: whilst she had an inkling of what had happened, the words hit like she was being stabbed all over again. Her heart raced as she realised she was in danger, but she could only weakly pull at the handcuffs. Her sister Sara pushed the woman with the GoPro to the ground.

"Stay the hell away from my sister!" Sara yelled at her. The woman simply got up and walked away with her hands in the air, dropping a handcuff key as she did. Sara picked up the key and freed a frightened Tegan who was trying her best not to hyperventilate. Sara placed the handcuffs to the side of Tegan's bed. Tegan started to hyperventilate in panic, upset at what she had learnt and scared of being hurt again. She felt as if even in her most vulnerable state, she wasn't safe. The two nurses started to try and calm Tegan down, moving Sara out of the way. A police officer approached Sara as a doctor went to help Tegan.

"Are you Sara Javaman?" the officer asked. Sara turned to face them, angry.

"Where the hell were you when a woman came in and handcuffed her just now? Are you seriously not going to do anything until my sister is dead?" Sara screamed at him.

"I understand you're frustrated Ma'am, but you need to calm down and have a chat with me," the officer tried to calm her down. Sara was about to scream at him again but she turned to face her sister who was highly agitated. She went back to Tegan who was starting to cry.

"It's okay, sister. No one's going to hurt you again, I promise," Sara said to Tegan, who wanted to believe her. She felt a little better knowing her sister was around but she couldn't help but feel she was putting Sara in harm's way again. The officer approached Sara again.

"Ms Javaman, we really have to talk," he said.

"Fine but under one condition: my sister has someone guarding her with only a set list of approved people allowed to visit her," Sara demanded as she faced him.

"Ma'am, I can't—" The officer started.

"My sister is a witness to a murder and the survivor of an attempted murder by someone who's been harassing her for weeks. It might be prudent for your investigation to keep her safe," she reasoned with them. The officer turned on their walkie talkie.

"Can we have an officer at Colton City Hospital please?" the officer spoke into their walkie talkie as they walked away. Sara went back to the foot of Tegan's bed as Tegan began to cry. She placed her hand on one of Tegan's covered feet.

"Tegan, I'm right here, love," Sara tried to soothe her as her little sister cried out.

Fear & Loathing

♥

It was now 2pm but to Tegan, it felt like forever had gone by since she learnt of Lloyd's death. She was wearing a nasal cannula instead of an oxygen mask. She was lying in her hospital bed, calm but emotionally numb. She fiddled with her blanket, having nothing else to move with her hands. She was staring at the ceiling, tempted to start counting the ceiling tiles to try and focus on something else. A police officer was standing by the entrance to the bay she was in, but she didn't feel much safer having them there. Darcy came through the ICU room and towards Tegan's bay. He was stopped by the police officer.

"Excuse me but you can't come in," the officer told him.

"My name is Dr Darcy Brandon. I'm here to see my colleague," Darcy told them. Tegan turned her gaze towards Darcy, pleased to see him even in her defeated and depressed state.

"Can I see some ID?" the officer demanded. Darcy showed him his hospital ID and the officer allowed him to pass. Darcy went straight to the side of Tegan's bed, relieved to see her awake and alive.

"Hey," he greeted her. Tegan flashed a small smile at him before reverting back to a more neutral expression.

"Hey," Tegan responded. There was a moment where she was unsure of what to say to him. She wanted to say so much to him and yet nothing at all at the same time. Tegan tried to bring herself up a little, but the pain of her wounds kicked in.

"Don't move if it hurts too much," Darcy told her kindly. "You're recovering."

"I thought you had work today?" Tegan asked innocently.

"You honestly thought I could go to work?" Darcy explained.

"What about Beth?"

"She's with Sinead and her daughter so I've got all the time in the world." Tegan continued to fidget with her blanket, unsure of what to say.

"I've got something for you," Darcy informed her. Tegan stopped fidgeting as he got something out of his pocket: a fidget spinner.

"It's not much. I got it from one of the shops here at the hospital. I know you like to fidget when you stim," said Darcy as he handed it to her.

"Thank you," she thanked him as she took the fidget spinner, touched by his thoughtfulness. She played with it a little before facing Darcy again. His hand was placed on the side of her bed.

"I'm sorry. I'm not very talkative right now," Tegan apologised.

"It's understandable. You've been through a lot," Darcy said.

"Sometimes it doesn't feel real. It's almost like it's a bad dream then I try to move, and it becomes clear how real it all is," Tegan explained. A brief silence fell between them as she struggled to know what to say. Tegan started to feel overwhelmed by her situation whilst tears welled in her eyes.

"I—" Tegan started as tears streamed down her face. "I never thought it would end up like this. Lloyd was a school crush who came back into my life. I knew Gabriella wouldn't take the breakup well but to kill—" She stopped as the gravity of what she was saying hit her like a tonne of bricks. She tried to stop crying but couldn't. Darcy grabbed a nearby box of tissues and tried to hand them to Tegan. She was too upset to think about the box of tissues in front of her. Darcy grabbed a tissue and dabbed her cheek gently. He tenderly dried her tears away until she calmed down and took the tissue from his hand.

"This isn't your fault, Tegan. None of it is," Darcy told her. Tegan looked down at her blanket and fiddled with it again.

"Would you like me to leave?" Darcy asked.

"No," Tegan told him as she stopped fiddling and placed her hand on his. "Stay. Please?" Darcy smiled at her and held her hand.

"I'll stay here as long as I can," Darcy agreed. He stroked her hand tenderly. Her heart raced as he touched her. She felt conflicted; on the one hand, she felt a sense of guilt for enjoying his affection but on the other, she craved this kind of attention more than anything else.

Several days passed with Tegan back at home for a little over a couple of days. She had largely kept confined to her bedroom upon her return. There was a darkness in her heart she couldn't quell. The guilt she felt for surviving Gabriella's attack and the fear of what might come next consumed her. The sound of Magda and Nadia coming up the stairs put her on edge. They both came to Tegan's bedroom door and knocked quietly.

"Tegan, do you want some lunch? You haven't eaten all day," Magda asked.

"No, thank you," Tegan replied.

"You need to get your strength back," Nadia tried to convince her.

"I said no," Tegan replied in a more firm manner. Nadia went back downstairs whilst Magda stayed by Tegan's door.

"Tigs, I know you must be feeling awful. I can't imagine what you're going through. Nadia and I only want what's best for you," said Magda. A part of Tegan wanted to respond, a part of her wanted to eat, and a part of her wanted to take comfort in those who cared about her the most but she didn't feel she deserved any of that. Her sense of self-hatred overrode her logical brain. She silently started to cry as she heard Magda walk away from her door. Tegan felt a whirlpool of negativity eat away at her as she desperately tried to stop crying. She felt that crying was a liberty she didn't deserve. She waited for the tears to stop streaming down her face. As they started to stop, someone knocked three knocks on the door. It spooked Tegan as it didn't sound like Magda nor Nadia's knocks. She slowly got up from her bed.

"Who is it?" Tegan asked.

"It's me," a familiar, silky smooth male voice uttered. Tegan felt incredibly conflicted; she didn't want to give in to her impulse to open the door but she didn't want to blow him off. She went to open the door but hesitated. Her heart pounded as she stood still in front of the door. Eventually, she opened the door. Darcy was standing there with a bunch of daffodils in a glass vase.

"May I come in?" he asked gently. Tegan stepped back, allowing him to come in. Darcy stepped in carefully and closed the door behind him. Tegan sat back on the bed, trying to make herself comfortable. Darcy placed the vase on the window sill.

"How's the wound?" Darcy asked as Tegan got herself comfortable.

"Fine," Tegan lied. Darcy approached her cautiously.

"You're a terrible liar. You look like you're in a lot of pain," Darcy said. "Have you been taking your painkillers?" Tegan looked away, ashamed.

"Why have you stopped taking them, Tegan?" Darcy continued. Tegan refused to answer, not wishing to give herself the gratification of potential help.

"I'm raising a teenage girl, the silent treatment won't work on me," Darcy said in a kind but firm tone as he sat on the end of the bed. A moment of silence befell the pair. Tegan started stimming by fiddling with her Fireman Sam t-shirt. Darcy smiled.

"I didn't think you were old enough for classic Fireman Sam," Darcy commented. Tegan faced him.

"My Dad used to show me old episodes when I was growing up," Tegan said, breaking her silence. Darcy smiled.

"Did you know that it was originally a Welsh language tv show?" Darcy informed her. Tegan shook her head.

"It's called 'Sam Tân' which I think translates to something like 'Fire Sam'," Darcy continued. Tegan flashed a smile but quickly retracted it. A feeling of guilt overwhelmed her because she dared to smile.

"Don't hide your smile, Tegan," Darcy tried to advise her.

"I don't deserve to smile," Tegan admitted. She continued to stim by fiddling with her t-shirt, trying to resist the urge to cry.

I Know You

❤

"Why don't you deserve to smile?" Darcy asked tenderly. Tegan looked at him intently. She didn't want to be questioned but she couldn't resist being somewhat honest with him.

"You know why," Tegan responded defensively.

"Okay I'll try this question: why are you not directing the anger at the person who deserves it most? Why are you taking it out on yourself?" Darcy tried again. Tegan turned her face away from him.

"You wouldn't understand." Tegan sighed.

"Then explain it to me."

"You want to explain it to you? Fine," Tegan snapped as she faced him again. "I made a stupid decision one night and it has followed me ever since. I already felt bad enough for kissing a man that was monogamously involved with someone else but clearly not bad enough to stop becoming involved with him the second he was available. Gabriella's hate campaign spread into every facet of my life all because I couldn't keep myself to myself. If I had shown some restraint, Lloyd might still be alive and I would still have both my ovaries." Darcy didn't speak for a moment which caused Tegan to secretly fear she'd put him off for good.

"Okay, you do realise you're wrong, right?"

"What would you know?"

"I know you, Tegan, better than most would think. You're a kind hearted person who tries so damn hard. You didn't deserve this. You didn't deserve for Lloyd to drag you into his mess, you didn't deserve Gabriella's relentless campaign, and you definitely didn't deserve to get stabbed. Could you have done things differently? Sure, but in the grand scheme of things, you're not the one who deserves punishment. Gabriella is and she'll get it one way or another." Tegan's eyes started to well with tears. Darcy's kindness was melting her hostile exterior.

"Please. Don't—" Tegan started as she tried not to cry.

"Don't what?"

"Be nice to me. You don't have to."

"I don't have to do anything. I chose to be here because—" Darcy stopped himself. He got a tissue out from his pocket and held it out for Tegan. This act of kindness broke her: her hard defensiveness melted away as she cried out. The strain of the past few weeks toppled her emotionally. She couldn't control herself anymore. Darcy approached her carefully on the bed and held her. She clung on to him as she continued to cry. He stroked her hair with his remaining hand with tenderness. For the first time since she was in the hospital, Tegan felt she had the right to do something other than self injury and the right to feel something other than overwhelming guilt. She felt the warmth of another human being comfort her.

Hours went by. Magda and Nadia were together in their living room, visibly wracked with anxiety. Nadia was stroking their cat Oedipus whilst Magda shook her legs so vigorously that it shook the sofa a little. Magda was consumed with worry for Tegan's behaviour and how that may impact her overall. The creak of the door opening stopped both Nadia and Magda in their tracks. Magda's anxieties fell away when Darcy and Tegan came slowly through the door. Tegan's arm was linked with Darcy's as he supported her.

"Tegan! You're out of your room!" Magda exclaimed.

"You need to eat something," Nadia remarked. Darcy guided Tegan to sit on the sofa next in between Nadia and Magda. Darcy sat on a nearby chair.

"I know. I shouldn't have anything too big," Tegan warned them.

"I've got some leftover chicken korma in the fridge if you want it, Tegan?" Magda offered.

"Honestly, I'd be happy with some toast and butter," Tegan admitted.

"Then I shall prepare that," Nadia said as they placed Oedipus back on the floor. They went off into the kitchen.

"Shall I get you a cup of tea?" Darcy offered Tegan. She smiled and nodded at him in acceptance of his proposal. He flashed a smile at her as he got up from his seat and followed Nadia into the kitchen. Tegan turned to Magda who gave her a knowing look. This perturbed Tegan slightly.

"What?" Tegan asked innocently.

"He's so into you," Magda declared.

"No he isn't," Tegan denied unconvincingly.

"Sorry, are we going to pretend that your kiss and everything before & after mean nothing?"

"No—"

"So, what's the problem?"

"What if it's all a bit too soon?"

"I'm not saying immediately marry the man. I'm just saying you should be truthful about your feelings towards him. You've been through enough rubbish lately so I'm sure he'll be respectful of whatever you choose to do," Magda reassured her with conviction. At that moment, there was a knock on the front door. Tegan became incredibly anxious and alarmed.

"Don't worry Tegan," Magda tried to soothe her. "I'm right here. No one's getting past me." They heard the front door open and the muffled sound of Nadia letting someone in. The door to the living room opened. Nadia came through with Darcy and a pair of police detectives. Darcy was holding a cup of tea in his hand.

"Tegan Javaman?" the first police detective asked.

"Yes?" Tegan responded tentatively.

"We're detectives Sweeney and Hallas. Do you remember us from the hospital?" the second detective asked as they both flashed their ID at her.

"Vaguely," Tegan answered suspiciously, unsure what was about to happen. Darcy went round to Tegan and placed the cup of tea on a coaster. He stayed close to her.

"We have some news for you. We managed to arrest Gabriella Stanford and her accomplice this morning," Detective Hallas informed the group. Tegan was shocked but relieved, so much so she began to cry again. Darcy placed his hand on Tegan's shoulder and Magda got some tissues from her pocket to hand to Tegan.

"Sorry," Tegan apologised. "I just—" Tegan struggled to talk through her tears.

"What happens next?" Nadia asked bluntly.

"They're both in cells at the moment but we are on route to interview them. Once they're formally charged, they'll be put in front of a magistrate court where they'll decide whether they get bail or not," Detective Sweeney answered.

"What are the chances of either of them getting bail?" Magda wondered, apprehensive to relax yet.

"That's not something we'll know until they get to the judge," Detective Hallas admitted.

"Does Tegan have to come to court?" Darcy asked in a concerned tone.

"No. We'll update Tegan throughout the process but if she wants to come to court, she's more than welcome," Detective Hallas informed the group. Tegan started to calm down as the information sunk in.

"Thank you. Did you want to stay for a cup of tea?" Magda offered graciously.

"Thank you but we do have to head off and interview the suspects. We just wanted to stop by," Detective Sweeney declined politely.

"Do you have any further questions?" Detective Hallas asked. Tegan dried the tears from her eyes and shook her head.

Another hour passed by. Tegan and Darcy were sitting together in the living room watching tv together. Darcy had his arm around Tegan, stroking her hair tenderly. Tegan felt a sense of safety she hadn't felt for a long time. Gabriella and her accomplice were locked away and Tegan was in an embrace with someone she felt deeply for. She felt as if things were almost perfect the way it was. Darcy's phone went off: he got a text from his sister, Beth. He checked it.

"It's Beth. I should go get her before it gets too late," Darcy told Tegan.

"That's fair enough. I can't have you all to myself," Tegan said in a joking tone.

"I'll be at work pretty solidly for a few days but I can swing by on my next day off," Darcy offered.

"Sure," Tegan agreed. Darcy helped Tegan up from the sofa. Once she was up, they found they didn't want to let go of each other. Darcy stroked her cheek as they looked into each others' eyes. In the moment, they felt powerfully drawn to each other. As their lips touched, they briefly hesitated before going in for the kiss. Their kiss was gentle and fuelled by mutual affection. As they withdrew from each other, they remained physically close.

"I think this means we need to talk," Tegan remarked, somewhat nervous of what might be said.

"I guess it does," Darcy agreed. Tegan took a deep breath as she prepared to be honest.

"I really like you," Tegan began. "I think you're an incredible person. My heart skips a beat whenever I see you. The safest I've felt has been when I've been with you. I want to be with you if you'll have me." Darcy couldn't help but smile at her words.

"You've been through a lot. I don't want to take advantage of you or your trauma because I really like you too. I want you to be sure," Darcy replied.

"I don't want a relationship yet, I need to pace myself. I do want to see where this goes. Does that make sense?"

"Yes. I want to take it slowly as well. You need to heal and I understand that. As far as I'm concerned, the ball is in your court. We'll go at your pace." The two smiled at each other and kissed each other again. The anxiety melted away as they embraced each other, safe in the knowledge they were on the same page. They reluctantly broke away from each other.

"I better get back to Beth. I'll let you know when I get home," Darcy said. Tegan nodded. As much as she didn't want him to go, she knew he had to.

"Okay. I'll have some more toast, take my painkillers then head back to bed. I'm pretty sore," Tegan admitted. Darcy stroked her cheek again and kissed her on the forehead.

"See you around," he coolly said as he left the house. As soon as she heard the front door close, Tegan smiled from ear to ear. She was elated at that turn of events, so much so that she could almost cry with happiness. Everything seemed to finally be turning around for her. Magda and Nadia came through the living room door together to see an elated Tegan.

"So?" Magda asked enthusiastically.

"We're seeing each other," Tegan confirmed. Magda, delighted for her best friend, hugged Tegan so hard it hurt her wounds. Tegan let out a loud cry.

"Magda, I love you but please don't do that again," Tegan complained. Magda quickly let go of Tegan.

"Sorry," Magda said.

"It's okay," Tegan forgave her friend.

"This is great. Gabriella is facing actual consequences, you and Darcy are together, and you're healing. Once you're off the painkillers, I say we should celebrate with some drinks," Nadia said in a celebratory tone.

"Maybe we should go back to The Shaky Martini." Magda suggested. Magda and Nadia started throwing date suggestions at Tegan but she was too happy to pay much attention. For the first time in a while, she felt content with her life: good friends, a solid man in her life, and a murderous enemy behind bars. What more could she ask for?

About the author

Jennifer Drewett is an author who writes about polyamory, neuro-diversity, disabilities, LGBTQ+ issues, and more. She has previously written articles for The Cosplay Journal and We Make Movies on Weekends.

Her debut book 'To Love At Comic Con' was released in 2022. She followed that up with a New Adult/Fantasy book 'New Leaves, Old Scars' in October 2024. Her latest book 'The Midwife in the Middle' released on Monday 28th July 2025. She is currently working on her next book.

She's been a writer for years having written articles, novels, and essays. Working a part time job in the NHS, she spends her free time looking for the next story.